I0581621

# BROKENHEARTED LOVE

# Brokenhearted Love

## Joann Buie

Independently published by Desert Wind Press LLC
www.desertwindpress.com

ISBN 978-1-956271-40-9 (paperback)

ISBN 978-1-956271-41-6 (ebook)

# CONTENTS

# Acknowledgments

Lori Hawkyard
Kevin Mead

and
to all the other friends and family
who have read my books. Thank you!!

# $\mathcal{P}$ROLOGUE

K atie's life was like a fast rolling roller coaster ride, but she learned to cope, found love, kindness, life and a real family that absolutely loved her.

In the beginning she couldn't wait to get out of work on Fridays, and get to the club so she could dance the night away. It seemed like she had lived solely for her Friday and Saturday nights anymore. With no ties to keep her at home, and when she was home during the week, all she thought about was going to the clubs. She needed to keep active.

Maybe she was thinking she'd meet her prince in shining armor or something like that fairy tale at the club, but it hadn't happened in the two years that she had been going there so that was a pipe dream down the toilet. She was what they referred to as a regular at the club with many friends, or so she thought. None of them ever asked her out on a date, or even out for a cup of coffee afterwards. Who was she kidding?

But it was better than spending her off time doing nothing because she didn't have anyone else to do anything with for starters. Going to the clubs was her social life, and she had a hard time thinking about quitting it all. Life would be a bore, and she didn't want that.

As she got ready to go to the club one night she had felt good about going. Didn't know why, but just a good gut feeling. As she walked in she started her rounds seeing the other regulars, and being politely nice to them. More and more friends were hooking up with other people with the group increasing in size, and in noise. She always ordered herself a large iced tea, and joined them in the area they always occupied.

Tonight there were a few new faces in the room. She caught the eye of one guy standing at the bar with probably a buddy of his watching the crowd as they danced. They'd laugh at times which had caught her attention, and the one guy had the greenest eyes she'd had ever seen. Good looking guy that wouldn't have a problem getting any girl in there to dance with him if he had asked.

It was half way through the night when that same guy came walking over towards the group, and asked her to dance with him. She was sure he had been heading their way for someone else, and couldn't believe he had picked her out of that group to dance with.

They walked out onto the dance floor hand in hand to dance. She had to admit that he was a great dancer. One dance led to another, then to another, and another.

In fact, it led to them dancing the rest of the night together. When the club was getting ready to close he had asked her out for a bite to eat afterwards.

She didn't even know his name yet, and wasn't about to go somewhere with a total stranger, and told him exactly that. He quickly grinned making a short laugh saying she was right, and promptly introduced himself as Matthew Jerome Milton doing a bow right there in the middle of the sidewalk where they had been standing. Katie laughed out loud adding that she was Katie, Katie Ann Kingsman as she did a curtsy, and decided it would be okay to go with him right there on the spot.

It was cold outside with the wind blowing hard. Snow was in the forecast, but it didn't matter to her. She felt plenty warm from dancing, and just talking with Matthew had kept the warmest feelings within her. They had walked a few places past the club to an all night diner where she had ordered a cheeseburger, fries, and the vanilla milkshake special. She had an appetite after all that dancing. Matt, as he preferred to be called, ordered the same. They sat there talking for over three hours about themselves, their jobs, and goals in life.

Katie was basking in all this because it was the first time she had been asked out after the club had closed for one thing, and that she had the attention of this man all to herself. It felt darn good.

Matt was in the military, was going to some sort of leadership skills school for six months, and just wanted to talk or write to someone while he was gone. Matt thanked Katie by kissing her on the cheek before they parted their ways.

Little did Katie know until the next afternoon that

he was friends with her ruthless mean spirited cousin Bradley, until she had gone to Brad's house for a get-together her Aunt Mary was having in Brad's honor. Brad was in the military also, and soon she learned it was the same place Matt would be going to with four others that showed up at Brad's party that afternoon.

Katie's life was going to be a roller coaster ride for sure, but one that she had stayed on until the end.

# Dancing Queen

⸺ ❧ • ◆ • ◆ ⸻

I was finally at home snuggled in my bed following a night to remember at the club, and the meeting of a wonderful guy named Matthew that I had danced with most of the night as well as going out for a bite to eat afterwards. I had the most marvelous time for the first time since I started patronizing that club. It was as if it had been meant to happen the way it had. I had been going to the same club for a few years, but after tonight I was sure glad I had never quit going. If I had quit I would have never met Matthew.

There were other clubs I could have gone to, but I knew my cousin Brad had frequently gone to those, and I definitely didn't want to be in the same place as him. I made that mistake once, and trust me when I say once was enough. When he spotted me there he had made nasty remarks loud enough for several people around us to hear. He had a knack of insulting me whenever he could when I got older.

He wasn't that way when we were kids, but once we were in high school the ugliness came out of him, and he never knew when to quit. Of course his buddies would laugh at everything he had to say, but he had really hurt me that one and only night at "his" club. I never brought it up to anyone what he had been saying, and I knew that he knew better than to say it, but it didn't matter to him. I knew things about his family that he would deny every word of if I were to tell things about him. I never did say anything, but there were times I wish I had the courage to say the few things that I did know.

I had a wonderful time that night dancing with Matthew. It was so hard to talk with him with the music playing as loud as it had been. Everyone had to scream over the next person to be heard, and I knew any talking would have to wait until later if he was still interested in talking to me. There were times when I thought the music would be lowered, but it didn't happen. Even though the slow songs could have been nicer with less volume you couldn't be heard no matter where you went, except maybe outside where it was freezing cold.

I was always particular in who I had danced with at the club, and when I left the place I always left with a group of people to be safe. I never had any problems, but there were a few of my friends that had experienced problems of high magnitude. It mostly involved the guys just fighting, but there were times when a girl had been accosted where the police had to be called, and arrests were made.

Most of the dance partners I had danced with at the

club just wanted to dance, and that was it. It didn't bother me much, but just once I would have liked to have had someone for more than a single dance every now and then. To me it wasn't fair, and the feeling of being used just to dance with a song of their choice, and on their terms just wasn't meaningful.

Matthew actually knew how to dance which was also very refreshing. He didn't just shuffle his feet from side to side like so many guys do, and letting their arms fling aimlessly in the air as if they were learning how to fly or something. That was so boring, and was rather embarrassing to me which I'm sure everyone had something to say behind our backs about. To me that wasn't what I considered dancing! But those guys thought they were so macho when it came to dancing that it didn't bother them. Matthew was definitely not like them. He was in total control of himself, and had some very nice dance moves. It made me feel great, and that in turn had made the night so special.

I also enjoyed the way Matt had held me in his arms on the slow dances. Close to him, but not the, "let go of me, I can't breathe", tight. Tender, but not sloppily loose, or have wandering hands that I had to fight off all the time. He was treating me with the utmost respect which I found to be rather nice.

When we had gone out for a bite to eat after the club had closed we talked for hours as if I had known him my entire life, but I hadn't which made what he said very interesting. All his topics were new, and refreshing compared to the local guys that came out to the clubs. All they seemed to know, and want to talk about were their so-called wonderful souped up cars. Most of their cars weren't all that nice, but you would have thought they just bought it at the Barrett-Jackson auction or something. I knew that immediately once I saw their cars that those guys were so full of it, and had no idea what a nice ride really looked like.

Matt was a kind guy that knew what he wanted in life, and how he was going to make it all happen. He was in the Army, and leaving in a few days for Leadership training in a school of some sort out of state. He had enlisted a few years back, and thought he'd make a career out of it. He liked what he was doing for the time being making decent money, but knew there would be times he would probably absolutely hate it, and wonder why he ever thought of making it a career. He was determined to make the best of everything the military had to offer though, and besides he had come this far already to not continue on.

His family didn't live too far from here either, just a few states away. He didn't talk much about them, and changed the topic stating that he was here for only a few days with a friend that was going to be deployed in a day or two overseas, so it wasn't important to talk about his family. It didn't sound like he was too interested in going home to be with his family for some reason, or talking about them, or maybe it was the bond the guys had when they were in the military looking out for one another. Military was their family in that aspect, and they considered themselves brothers. Matt didn't say why he felt the way he did about not going to see his parents and family, and at the time it really didn't matter to me. I wouldn't have met him if he had gone home for one thing!

He asked if he could write to me when he was gone, and asked if I would write back. Said the guys live for letters from people back home all the time to make their deployment a little more tolerable, if that was ever possible. I didn't have anything to lose by writing to him, so I agreed to it figuring that he would probably find someone else on his next adventure, and soon he'd forget about me. I was okay with that because I knew how guys like to talk the talk, but not able to walk the walk when it had involved me. My past experiences made me keenly aware of that. But for now it was a good idea, and maybe he was sincere in what he was saying. Time will only tell.

I was completely exhausted from my night out with Matt when I got home, and fell in bed for a few hours of sleep before having to get up to go to my cousin's house for the get-together my aunt was throwing for him. My dear aunt…. she means well I suppose, but I think she does it more for herself than for anyone else. I don't think she thinks things completely through at times which has come back to bite her, but it never seems to bother her that much. Just flies by the seat of her pants more than anything. I do know that she thinks everyone in town are her close friends. I noticed the same ones come to all her parties, but she never seems to get invited to their place for some strange reason. I consider them her fair weather friends, and I wish my aunt would open her eyes to see it for herself, but she never does. She thinks they just can't make a party as interesting as she can, and when it comes to throwing a party she goes all out. My aunt involves them with everything she does, or has to say. I think most of them are barflies that gather at the bar she frequently goes to with my mother. The bar is where my mother meets most of her friends that she seems to always drag home.

Her son Bradley, is in the Army as well, and just finished some sort of training before he is heading somewhere else for a few months. Aunt Mary was so proud of him as she should be, but thinks he is someone extra important in the military, and wanted all her friends to see him off. I think this "get-together" was more for Aunt Mary to brag about Brad one last time than what it was for him. But either way the invite was there, and I was expected to attend. If I had anything else planned I would have had to change them to be at her party.

Brad always went along with his mother's plans, whether he wanted to or not. He lived for the attention people gave him just as much as Aunt Mary gobbled it up for herself. I wouldn't be surprised if he would be wearing his uniform for this get-together to show off even more. He definitely was an attention seeker. With his mother the way she was it really didn't surprise me either. The apple didn't fall far from that tree for sure in that aspect.

Brad was just a few years older than me. He was always nice to me when I was around as a kid only because he had to be. Several times he got stuck with me tagging along with him and his friends which he didn't seem to mind that much…. I don't think anyways. I know I didn't mind tagging along with him and his friends. They did the fun things that I would have never dreamed of doing myself. Some of the things I thought were rather dangerous, but I did them anyhow. It made me feel like one of the guys when I could do everything without being scared.

Brad could also be really really mean towards me at times, too. I knew he was angry several times when I showed up ruining his time with his buddies, and had taken it out on me. But all in all I had survived being with him, and his friends.

We always had fun when we were small, but as we grew older the novelty wore off, and I also didn't need to have someone watch over me like that anymore. It was just a ploy so my mother and aunt could talk without us around to overhear their conversations, or to bother them. The part of growing up that seemed so unfair to me. Getting pushed aside by Brad, and my own mother was hard to swallow at times, but I made the best of it. I would just bring a book with me to read outside under the willow tree in their backyard when we went to their house. Too old to tag along, and too young to join in on the women talk. I was stuck no matter what.

During the summer months I would house-sit for Aunt Mary while she traveled all over the world. She would meet up with people at some of the strangest places, and visit places that I could only dream about. The amount of money she spent traveling was an obscene amount, but she would chuckle saying most of her expenses were paid for by the many friends she would meet along the way which were mainly male friends. I could only guess what kind of friends they were. She was a young looking beautiful middle aged woman that didn't have a care in the world. No husband to bother her, and now no child left at home that she had to tend to. She was free to go, and do as she wanted for as long as she wanted. Be the free spirit. I guess it makes her happy, and that's all that matters to her.

I had planned on house-sitting that summer since I have the summers off with my job as a teacher assistant at the elementary school in town. I needed the little fill-in jobs to keep a nice flow of money coming in. My aunt didn't pay the greatest amount, but it was better than nothing. I had plans for my money, and the more I made the sooner I could make my plans come true. I wanted to leave this town, and be away from the drama, and my family.

I had a small apartment in town within walking distance to my job at the school which was very convenient for me. The place had been a huge Victorian house that had been converted into four tiny apartments over the years. I had the front upstairs apartment that was a single bedroom, bath, kitchen with a very compact eating area, pantry closet, and rather large living room which was perfect for me. I had my furniture arranged to consume the rooms without it looking crowded, or spaced too far apart. My desk was in there, and a card table set up for my jigsaw puzzles I'd put together to keep me from getting totally bored when the weather was bad. It was homey, and I was pretty comfortable being there. I felt it was safe from being broken into while I was house-sitting for my aunt. The other renters were older, and usually very nosy by watching everyone come and go like they did.

I was lucky to find that apartment when I did with the rent being ridiculously cheap. The owner had made enough money off the larger apartments he could afford to take less for a single bedroom one. Most people wanted nothing less than two bedrooms, but I didn't need a second bedroom so I moved in, and was happy as a clam. I think Mr. Smitt was relieved when I took it. It had sat empty for several years being used as a catch all room, and he said he could rent it to me for a little less, and that he wouldn't have to keep advertising it anymore.

My windows were the old floor to ceiling type where I could see everything going on in the front of the place, and down the street in both directions when I looked out. Lots of natural light came through those floor to ceiling windows.

I had all new furniture delivered the day I had moved in. I always heard the phrase that it only costs a little more to go first class. That way everything I had purchased would be a perfect fit for the space I wanted it in. And, I didn't want my first apartment to be loaded with things that I had to settle for. I had lived like that all my life with everyone else's hand me downs, and I wanted something new, and nicer than I had growing up. I was pleased that everything was mine, and it was all new, and completely paid for. I had saved my money for it with the part time job I had in high school, and the job I had at the school being a teachers assistant for the past two years. I just knew I needed to move out of my mothers home to start my own life, and everything has worked out as I had planned, so far.

Plans? That was as far as I got with making my plans and goals at least for another year. I had none other than working all week, going out to clubs on weekends, stay out as long as I wanted with no one else to answer to, or have to hear any lectures on my life style. What a life I thought I finally had, huh!

I arrived at Aunt Mary's house for the get-together

later that day, and there were cars parked all over the place. I thought she said there would only be a few close friends, not the entire town. I had to walk what seemed liked a mile after I had parked my car just to get to her house. I was glad there wasn't any snow to walk through. The roads were clear, but the temperatures were still low with the wind blowing to remind us who was boss on days like these. The dark clouds showed promise of a cold night ahead with possibly of some snow. I just hope it held off until I was back home.

I greeted Aunt Mary as soon as I walked in, and sought out Brad to wish him well once the crowd around him had tapered off. I was right too, he stood there proudly wearing his Army uniform with his chest puffed out in pride. What a character he was. I couldn't believe he had joined the Army though. That was the last thing I ever expected from him. He wanted to travel to see the world like his mother, and I guess he thought this was the way to go, and still get paid for doing it. I wonder if he thought it was going to be a vacation while in the Army.

My mother was on the far wall surrounded by several of her male friends from the bar where she spends way too much time as far as I was concerned. I'm sure she never even noticed me when I waved to her, or maybe she was just ignoring me. Either way I wouldn't have any contact with her while she was with those kind of friends. They gave me the creeps just looking at them. I thought I'd be able to talk to her later, but she was pretty content being the center of attention in her little group. Yes, she certainly had the attention from several guys with her short red dress that had hiked it's way up even further on her thigh, and the low cut top exposing her breast easily. She was probably three sheets to the wind by this time. I laughed to myself thinking more like the whole wash, not just three sheets!

I use to think she was such a beautiful person, and she really was. She dressed to the nines all the time, and most of my friends thought she looked like a movie star when we were young. I was pretty proud of her, and many times I thought I wanted to be just like her. I had basked in the compliments my friends had said to me about her beauty. I'd smile at them, and when my mother would hug me I was happy because I knew that they knew I was her daughter.

It wasn't until I was in junior high school that I started to understand what the boys were saying about her. It wasn't nice, but they were only repeating what they had heard their fathers say. I didn't like it. Several times I'd try to defend my mother, and it only made things worse for me. When I told my mom what they were saying she didn't seem to be bothered by it. She would tell me their father's had little room to be talking about her. She seemed to know the father's on a first name base some how. I started to understand everything then, and that was when I knew I didn't want to be like her at all.

I didn't want to believe that what was being said could possibly be true, but the more I thought about it, the more I realized it probably was. I was so hurt that my mother would act the way she did around men, and dress the way she had. She was far from any movie star status that I could think of. And she didn't seem to understand how it was affecting me personally with the guys at school. It was so hurtful to know what people were saying about her. Some of the guys were just down right nasty to me. I knew I would either have to move away when I got older, or change my name. I didn't want anyone to know that I was related to her. I sure hated the fact that my mother's life style made me negative about her more and more.

Several months later my mother had asked me why I had changed. I couldn't get it through to her that her bad reputation was drifting down to me, and how people were saying things, and judging me for her actions. She had been so pretty at one time, but now she wasn't as pretty, or as nice. She was mainly drunk most of the time staying hours on hours in a bar hooking up with guys.

I don't know how many times I was left alone at night so she could have her "fun", and where I would cry myself to sleep hoping and praying that she would stop it all, and be a good mother to me. It didn't happen no matter how much I had pleaded with her. I had even offered to help her quit that life style. She informed me that she didn't want to change her life style, and that I needed to mind my own business. That was when I decided as soon as I graduated from high school I would find a place for myself. That I did do, and so glad I had.

I had been told by her that she didn't need me to report back to her as she waved her hand like it was nothing. After all, she was a big girl now, and knew what she was doing. She didn't care if she ruined someone's marriage or not, and she didn't care if she had to be driven home because she was too drunk to drive. But I cared!! The kids in school knew I belonged to her, and had whispered behind my back loud enough for me to hear several times. It was embarrassing and hurtful that my own mother didn't care how it looked to anyone let alone me.

Just as I was about done talking with Brad I had someone tap my shoulder from behind me. I quickly turned around to see who it was. It was Matt from the night before. He was Brad's friend, and the Army buddy he would be seeing the world with once he was out of his training and leadership school. Who would have thought that? I had never put two and two together last night when he told me about being in the Army. Why would I? Many people enlist into the Army.

Brad was just as surprised when he found out that I was the same person that Matt had been bragging about meeting at the club the night before had been me, his own cousin. That was all I needed. My cousin to interfere in my life over his buddy. I played it off as if it wasn't a big deal, but deep down I was really glad to see Matt once again. I think Matt even sensed my feelings at that time, and went along with what I was saying, by not going into the fact we stayed out until four this morning just talking. I'm sure Brad would have made something out of it, or give me a lecture over something that was none of his business.

Brad wouldn't let it go though, and he kept hammering us for more and more details. It got so bad that I was feeling uncomfortable talking with either one of them. I politely excused myself to go mingle with other people that I knew. I did keep my eye on Matt although I'm sure he would soon be having second thoughts of talking anymore to me. I could probably forget about getting any of those letters from him, too. I couldn't wait until I could politely leave this get-together, shindig, or whatever they were calling it, and forget everything that happened the past two days. I was feeling pretty miserable by then, and the only way to leave politely was to lie saying I wasn't feeling well which I did. Aunt Mary hugged me saying she hoped I wasn't coming down with anything contagious, and went directly back to her friends within seconds of talking to me.

By the time I reached my car I was freezing cold, and close to tears. How could Brad be so cruel to me when Matt had come over to talk to me? Brad wasn't my older brother looking out for me. Not by a long shot. I was a grown woman, and I could handle my own affairs without him meddling in my life. He certainly didn't have any room to judge the company I kept. I knew who he had spent times with in the past, and they weren't the kind he'd likely introduce his mom to. That was for sure! But I never said a thing to anyone about those shady women he had entertained.

By the time I got home I was a hot mess from over thinking everything that had happened. Before I got out of the car I let the tears fall. I don't know why I cried the way I had. Maybe it was from the lack of sleep, I don't know. Was it because of Brad's badgering questions, or because I probably would never hear from Matt again? I didn't know. All I knew was that I was feeling rather crappy at the moment, and just wanted to be left alone.

My mother would have had a hissy fit if she saw me right now. She always thought there was an "image" to protect, and this would not be a part of it. I didn't care, and besides, no one could see me in my car anyhow. What does she know about having a bad experience like that. She had told me over and over of all the fun times she had growing up, and all the parties she had been invited to, to the many boys in her life. She had stated she had a line of them just waiting to date her. She made me feel as if there was something wrong with me more often than not, because that hadn't happened for me the same way it did for her. Made me wonder what all she had done to get those many dates she highly bragged so much about. I could only guess, and I can bet my guesses were probably right!

My mom did like to socialize a lot, and she always had men flocking to her. I think that was the reason her and my dad had divorced when I was so young. Just having parents divorced was bad enough for me growing up, but to have my mother's actions talked about around town was horrifying to me. That was the main reason I wasn't the social butterfly as she thought she was. I didn't want to have people gossip about me like they did her.

I couldn't even call my dad to get his advice on anything either, when I needed it the most. He had remarried a few years after their divorce, and he had a whole new family. He didn't want the "old family" to mingle with his new family which included me. That was another blow to my confidence that I had a hard time dealing with. I had a father that wasn't a father to me in terms that I had to accept at a very young age.

One last sob and I was ready to go inside to get under my covers, and go to sleep. Sleep? I don't think I was able to get more than a few minutes here and there as everything kept going through my mind. By the time I finally got up it looked like the covers on my bed had been through the war zone itself. I had even managed to pull the bottom sheet corners up exposing the bare mattress. I know all I did was toss and turn, but that was ridiculous. And my poor pillow was out of shape with the pillowcase covered with the black mascara I hadn't washed off from the night before.

I remembered several of my dreams I had during the night. They were mostly a rehash of what had happened at Aunt Mary's, and that to me was more of a nightmare than a dream. I decided I wasn't going to let it get to me, and I was not going to think about it anymore. I decided that I'd keep my distance from everyone the next few days until the whole ordeal passed. The story of my life was having to "let things pass".

I was the one who always had to let things pass. No one else would take their actions seriously which in turn reflected onto me, but they didn't care. I was always told, "it'll pass", and left with that message ringing in my ears far too many times. Well, things did pass over, but only after I had to endure the ridicule for a few days in school. It was hard to hold my head high, to endure it all, but I somehow managed. I had built a wall of stone around myself trying not to allow the hurt I felt to destroy me. Even though I had let things pass I could always forgive, but never could I forget.

I had showered and dressed before I made my bed, and fixed myself breakfast. I didn't feel much like eating so I found a pack of Instant Breakfast that I mixed with cold milk. It filled me, and I was feeling better.

I had been lazy around the apartment all morning not knowing what I planned to do when there was a knock at my door. I really didn't want to see anyone, and got as quiet as I could so whomever it was would just leave thinking no one was home. Unless it was Mr. Smitt who would just use his set of keys to open the door anyhow.

Well, whomever it was didn't leave, and knocked again and again. Louder each time until I knew I better open it before my neighbors heard the commotion, and got mad. I looked through the door peep hole to see who it was, and I heard Matt's voice pleading with me to open the door allowing him to come in. He needed to talk to me, and it couldn't wait. Matt?? How did he know where I lived?? And which apartment I lived in?? What the heck was going on?

# A Special Weekend

◆

**M**y heart sank. I reluctantly opened the door ever so slightly, but not wide enough for him to come in. I didn't want him to come in, and I really didn't want him to stay long enough to talk either. I knew where I stood with Brad and his buddies now, and I didn't want anything to do with any of them. Brad had made that crystal clear last night at his party which had made me look like a foolish loser to everyone there.

The look on Matt's face was a look of grief as he spoke to me as if he had been caught with his hand in the cookie jar. He had gotten my address at Brad's house by snooping in Aunt Mary's address book she had by the phone while no one was looking. He said he had to see me to talk about what had happened because he felt horrible the way Brad had spoken to me, and with all the questions he had demanded answers to, which Matt could tell that it had made me very uncomfortable. Brad's other buddies were also interested in what was happening that they came over to add their two cents as well without knowing anything of importance, and actually encouraged Brad to humiliate me as long as he possibly could. Everyone but Matt had been enjoying it too much, and I knew I couldn't take Brad berating me much longer before I would end up making a complete fool of myself by blowing up at him. That would have added more fuel to the fire that was already burning intensely on me, and why everyone needed to just stay away.

Matt knew I had been embarrassed, and justifiably hurt. I had turned to walk away before Matt could stop it from going on any longer, but I felt that it was a little too late. I didn't know what Matt was trying to do at that moment, but I wasn't going to be an easy target for him, for Brad, or for any of Brad's loyal subjects. My life would go on as it always had, and I would have been played as another fool of Brad's devilish encounters. Heck, I was use to that, but I had felt there had been something special about Matt. Whenever it came between me or Brad, he always won hands down. I could never put him in his place where he belonged no matter how hard I tried, so I did the best thing I could do by leaving.

I could only guess what had transpired after I had left between Brad and Matt, but I didn't want to go there questioning Matt like Brad had done to me. If Matt had wanted me to know what had happened he would have to tell me.....I wasn't going to pry. That was Brad's area of expertise.

Since I didn't want any of my neighbors knowing my

business that we were discussing in the hallway I finally opened the door allowing Matt to enter. I quickly offered him something to drink hoping if it was bad news for me that he would choke on it. All he wanted was a glass of water which I got for him, and showed him to the living room so he could sit down. He sat on the couch, and I purposely sat on the love seat away from him as I stared intensely at him boring a hole into his soul. He finally spoke to me after a few sips of water. He didn't choke, but I noticed how much his hands were shaking while holding that glass.

I asked Matt what brought him to my place because I was under the understanding that Brad had made it crystal clear yesterday that he didn't want any of his buddies to be involved with me. It had really made me mad that Brad could manipulate me in that way, and some of his friends the way he had. Even more so that I didn't put a stop to his berating me the moment he started by simply walking away sooner than what I had. No courage from me there what-so-ever. But I knew I had better not say anything at all. I had lived through the wrath of Brad in the past for doing that….barely, and it wasn't nice nor easy.

The moment Matt had walked past me to take his seat in the living room. I could easily smell his cologne once again. It took me back to the night before when I had first met Matt at the dance club. We must have sat there looking at each other for several minutes before Matt finally started telling me how sorry he was at how Brad was such a jerk towards me yesterday. It was none of Brad's business who he saw, and more importantly who I saw. He wasn't going to leave things hanging the way they were because he thought it was rather crappy what Brad had done and said. And to think Brad could demand that his buddies stay away from me was over the limit. He was really sorry, and expressed how he should have stood up to Brad immediately, but we both knew it would have made matters worse for both of us, especially for me, and Matt didn't want that.

Matt had looked for me after I had left the group so we could talk alone, but he couldn't find me anywhere. He had finally asked my Aunt Mary where I could be, and she had told him I wasn't feeling well so I had left as she went back to talking with her friends. He knew I wasn't sick as in the throw up kind of sick, but probably extremely upset with Brad, and he didn't blame me for that one bit. No one saw him look through the address book next to the phone, and he didn't care if anyone had seen him because he had wanted to find me. He couldn't let things be the way they had happened.

Matt had wanted to see me to get to know me better without stepping on Brad's toes or listen to his controlling demands, and if that wasn't possible, it was too bad for Brad. Matt said he had such a great time dancing at the club with me, and going out to eat afterwards that he couldn't leave things the way it had ended. He hadn't had such a great time in several years stating that he was truly glad he had met me. But he also had a rotten time trying to fall asleep last night thinking about what all had happened, and what Brad had said afterwards about me being such a loser. Good ole Brad to think that much of me, and especially bold enough to make those statements to his buddies.

I didn't know what to say, but I could feel my heart

beat a little faster than what it had yesterday after leaving the get-together/party or whatever it was being called. I told him I was shocked to learn that Brad and Matt had known each other because I felt they were such a complete mismatch as friends. Such a small world when you think about it. I told Matt I was so upset that I had to get out of there as soon as possible, and left when no one was paying attention to anyone else, but to dear ole Brad. Brad definitely had the attention from everyone, and had basked in it as much as he could. That was the way he was. He knew he could never do anything wrong in his mom's eyes. Such arrogance!!

I had to lie about not feeling well to get away from his party. Actually I didn't feel well. I was having a start of a full blown panic attack, and knew I needed to get out of there before it escalated any more than what it already had. I didn't want to make a fool of myself crying in front of anyone, and I definitely didn't want to let Brad know that he had the power to control me the way he thought he could.

Matt had totally agreed by replying that he wished he had known what happened to me. He said he saw me talking with another couple one minute then gone the next. No one had seemed to know where I had gone to, and that was when he saw Aunt Mary's address book next to her phone. He looked under the K's, and I was the only one written down so he tore the whole page out of her book, and a little later left himself hoping he would be able to find me. Apparently no one had seen him leave the party either which he was glad about.

Not knowing the town very well, and with it being late at night he didn't have any luck finding my street. So he waited until today when he could see the street signs better and voila, he found me. At least he had hoped he was banging on the right door when he arrived.

I eased up on my mistrust of him as we sat there talking more about ourselves, family, and jobs. Just like it had been before Brad's party. Neither one of us had eaten lunch yet, and it was already close to one so we decided to go out for lunch. We also went to a see a movie I had been wanting to see. As it turned out, Matt had the same taste in music, literature, and movies as me. My afternoon was looking better by the minute. I felt pretty sure no one would see us at the movies in the dark, and was quite sure Brad was probably hung over from drinking as much as he did at his party. He definitely liked his beer, and always drank too much.

We found a small diner open by the theater, and went in there. We had more than enough time before the movie started to eat, and I had to admit that I was pretty hungry. I ordered their special cheeseburger, fries, and iced tea to drink knowing I wanted to save room for the popcorn while watching the movie. I just can't go to the movies without getting their snacks for some reason. Especially their hot buttered popcorn. That aroma hits you smack in the face as soon as you enter the theater making you desire a bag full.

During the movie our hands went for popcorn at the same time, and before I knew it, we were watching the rest of the movie while holding hands. I wasn't sure if I should have pull away at that time, or just let it ride. I had decided to let it ride, and I felt pretty special on the inside that my hand was perfectly nestled in his.

We chatted about the movie all the way back to my

place afterwards. Once at my apartment I invited him back in, but he said he had to get going. It was getting late. I didn't want the night to end just yet. When he asked me if he could come by again tomorrow I tried not to sound too eager by answering him that I would like that very much, so I just nodded a yes to him. He gently brought my face toward his face bringing his mouth to mine as he kissed me good night. I thought my knees were going to buckle under me right then and there. And then he was quickly gone leaving me standing at my door touching my lips with my fingers as I smiled.

Early the next morning Matt had called asking me if I'd like to go to lunch, and for a ride in the country with him. I was glad that he had called, and had accepted the chance to be with him again. I knew this would be his last day there as he had to be back at the base, but I had wanted to see him one last time before he left.

When he picked me up he had told me he had rented a cabin for the day in the country where we could ice skate on the pond, and we could eat lunch nearby if that was okay with me. The first time a guy asked me if I was okay with a plan, and it was rather nice. I looked forward to the day events, but I didn't look forward to when he had to leave. Bittersweet feelings were rushing through my head already.

The little cafe where we ate was quaint, and had delicious food. I had never been there before, and I thought I had been to all the places to eat in this town and the outskirts, but I missed this one some how.

The cabin was absolutely beautiful and overlooked the frozen pond. That pond was huge! There were other people ice skating already. A little building by the pond had skates available with hot chocolate and tiny powdered donuts for their guests. We hurried down to the pond to put on our skates, and was soon skating our afternoon away. I knew my face was red from the cold because it was stinging, but I was not cold myself. Matt and I held hands as we skated around the pond, and several times he would twirl me around him like a pro-skater would. We skated as if we had skated all our lives together without missing a single stride. I enjoyed skating for the first time since I was much younger.

Back at the cabin we enjoyed a movie after we popped popcorn in the fireplace and warmed ourselves. I was snuggled in Matt's arms through the entire movie. Little did I know that Matt had also ordered dinner to be delivered to the cabin from that little cafe before we had left there earlier in the day. He set the table in front of the huge window facing the pond adding long tapered candles for a centerpiece. It was the most romantic time I have ever had on a date, and I was enjoying everything about it.

Driving back to my apartment we had talked about how we would like things to go from here on out for the both of us, and if there was a chance on us as a couple. Matt wanted to be sure I would answer his letters as much as I wanted him to write to me. We had a great thing going for us in such a short amount of time, and I knew then I had feelings for him already. Maybe it was too soon, but I was feeling them. The feelings were taking over my body in warm sensational waves. I was concerned that it might be premature to feel this way after the losers I have had in my life, but this was absolutely wonderful.

It was hard to say goodbye to Matt when he had to leave that night. I didn't want the night to end or have him be gone for a whole six months, but we knew he had to go. He reached over to kiss me good night. It was the best kiss ever until the second kiss and then the third. I could have kissed him all night.

I walked with him to the outer door of the apartment place, and watched as he got in his truck to drive away. I was really surprised when I realized I had tears in my eyes. I had never had that happen before, but that was the way I was feeling right then. It was pure sadness. Very sad. Everything had come to an end so soon, and I didn't really know if it was a permanent end or not. I felt in my heart it was the beginning of something wonderful, but I also had to face reality that it might be just a weekend fling filled of fun. Only time will tell how it goes.

I thought maybe I should call Brad to wish him well before he left, but decided against it. He didn't deserve it as far as I was concerned. I thought maybe if I didn't call him that he'd realize he had over stepped his bounds with me. I had other things to think about and do, and they didn't include him. I wasn't going to let Brad make anymore comments to me to ruin how I was feeling at the moment. I knew he would if I had called, so why should I set myself up to that?

I also had a hard time sleeping that night as I kept thinking about Matt, and how wonderful I felt when he was around. I would write to Matt every day if I had to, and wait to see if I'll actually ever see him again, and go from there. I do hope I see him this summer when he finishes his training. Who knows where he'll be stationed after that, but most likely it will be under

Brad's supervision. I think this training Matt had to do was so that he would be in that deployment group with Brad overseas.

I probably should have asked Matt if it would be, but I never thought about it until then. I was only thinking about me and Matt at that moment, and Brad was the last thing I wanted to think or talk about right then.

I was in seventh heaven when I received my first letter from Matt a few days later. He told me everything that was happening at his leadership school, and yes, he would be in the same squadron at Brad once he completed his training. Brad was so full of himself all the time. A real showboat was what Matt had called him, and I knew Matt was right about that. The guys would do all the grunt work, and Brad would take all the recognition for it. Yep, that was the way Brad was. Me, me, me!!

The guys will get their cell phones back in about two more weeks so Matt will be able to call or text me then. Until then he wanted me to know how much he enjoyed his weekend with me, and that he was thinking of me all the time. How sweet could that be, and how good it had made me feel whenever I thought about it which was all the time.

Matt said he was all for the military life, and planning on making it a career. He hinted that he had wished that his family would understand, but they weren't too keen on his choice. In fact, he hadn't heard a word from any of them since he had enlisted. He didn't seem too upset over it, but he would have liked to have had a letter from them now and then. He had done his part at writing to them explaining what he was learning, and how important it was. Important not only to him, but to the country as well.

They had expected him to live at home helping them with everything after he had graduated from high school. He knew that he had to leave. He wasn't supporting them or their bad habits any longer. He wanted to make more of his life than what he had seen in his future by staying there. When the recruiter came to the school on career day to talk to potential soldiers, Matt knew exactly what he was going to do after listening to him.

Matt had said his parents were really mad at him when he told them that he had enlisted, and was leaving for boot camp the day after graduation. They were so mad that they kicked him out of their house before school had ended, and he slept in his truck until graduation. What a rotten way to remember his senior year and his graduation! Maybe sometime down the road his family might understand why he chose the military for his future. I know that he would of liked to leave with their full support, but it wasn't going to be.

I couldn't wait to write back to him. I had purchased a nice box of stationary on my way home from work the other night to write my letters on. It wasn't feminine or anything that would attract any attention to his letters. Just plain beige paper with gold scrolls across the top. Very masculine if I do say so myself.

# SCHOOLS OUT

I started receiving text messages from Matt shortly after the guys got their cell phones handed back to them, and I answered him immediately. Most of my texts came through in the early evening. Matt had said Brad had been avoiding him much of the time, or giving him salty looks for some reason, but never talking to him. Matt was going to talk to him to get things cleared up about what was bugging him, or let him know their friendship was over outside of the work place.

Work was going great at school, and I was able to sock away more money from every paycheck. I wasn't out clubbing as often as I had in the past, and left at a decent hour on the few times I had gone. I just didn't enjoy being there without Matt anymore, and I was happy to see how much money I had been able to save by not going there. I didn't have anyone I wanted to dance with that held a spark to Matt, and my friends were just fair weather friends as I found them to be. They never even realized I hadn't been going after a while. A real friend would have asked where I had been but nothing from them at all. That was when I realized I was just a body in their little group, and nothing more.

My nights seem to drag on longer than I liked after texting or talking to Matt. Many times he couldn't call, and I missed hearing from him. Just hearing his voice made my days so much nicer. Those were the days that I worried that something bad had happened. Sometimes he could text only a few sentences, but I was glad to hear something from him. People might think I was crazy to have this long distance friendship going since we were in different states, but it felt good to me, and for the first time I felt like it was the real deal.

I lost interest in my jigsaw puzzles so I put them back in their boxes, and donated them to the senior center in town. I can only clean my tiny apartment so many times. It was ridiculous how much time I had wasted on the phone talking to friends, or clubbing in the past. I had a sick feeling that these next six months were going to drag by slowly for me.

The weather had turned bitterly cold suddenly. I looked out the window to the street below noticing that very few cars were traveling on it. At least people were smart enough to stay off the streets in this weather. The houses had their lights on, but the glow they gave off was dim, and rather sad looking. I finally settled for another movie, and fell asleep while watching it. It wasn't that interesting to begin with, but I thought it would help get the night over with. I just stayed covered up on the couch with my electric blanket trying not to think too far into the future.

Matt had talked to Brad, and point blank asked him why he was being such a jerk to him lately. Brad was still mad at him because of me and Matt being together at the club as well as his send off party. He didn't like that idea at all. Thought it was rude of us to be there together.

Rude?? We weren't the ones who made a jerk of ourselves, he was the one that had done that. There was nothing Brad could do about it. Brad stated that he didn't think I would like being on the waiting end of visits from Matt, or the possibility of us making a go of it. Matt told Brad that I wasn't made from the same cloth as my mom, but Brad must have had other thoughts concerning that. He told Matt that staying faithful in my family was a joke. He was concerned that I wouldn't be able to wait for him, that I would most certainly break his heart, and he couldn't have a troop in the field with that kind of deceit clouding his mind.

I really think Brad was just upset that he had no control over either one of us, and that was the root cause of his bad attitude. Brad had never had a decent relationship with any girl from the time he started dating in high school up to now. I really think the girls got tired of Brad's garbage, and would dumped him as soon as possible. But the way Brad talked you'd would have thought it was the other way around. Of course he didn't want anyone to think he had been dumped. Heavens no! That would make people second guess him about other things he bragged about as well. He had a reputation to keep. He thought he was all that even back then, so why should I think he had changed by going into the military?

Matt had told him we were keeping in contact with each other, and that he planned to see me as often as he could whether it made him happy or not. Brad wasn't giving me any credit for picking out guys in the past, and felt this was just another failure. That wasn't what Matt needed to hear even though it was true. I never had a relationship lasting longer than a month, and that was what Brad had told Matt. Brad told Matt to be aware when the month comes around because it would be here before long, and I would be dumping him for better fish in the ocean, or visa versa. Matt said he didn't buy any of the crap Brad had said. Matt said he would know when things aren't going well between us, and if it ever came to that we'd talk through it. We were adults, and that's what adults do.

Brad didn't know any of the reasons behind my breaking up with any of the other guys either. I couldn't tell him that they were jerks, and made me feel uncomfortable being with them. One date had me so upset when I stopped him from going too far that he told me to get out of his car, and I had to walk home. It was a long way home for me to walk, and he didn't have a second thought about me making it home safely. Several of those dates were his best buddies in high school, and they could do no wrong in Brad's eyes. I didn't have any trust with them where Matt was so different. He wanted to get to know me for me, and we had a great time getting to know each other first.

I wrote a letter to Brad telling him that he needed to butt out of my life when it came to the guys I dated. He wasn't in charge of me. I had grown since all those other guys were a part of my life. I had also grown up for the better, living on my own, making better decisions and choices, and not following in my mother's footsteps. I was completely different from my mother in so many ways. I was livid with Brad, and knew it might end his friendship with Matt. Matt wasn't too concerned with that happening. I set the letter on the table to mail in the morning, but by morning I had decided against dropping it in the mailbox. I decided I just wasn't going to let Brad know anything about how I felt, what I was doing, and my contact with Matt. This was just his way of pushing my buttons to get a reaction out of me. Brad wasn't worth the time or energy I had spent writing it, and I tore the letter up throwing it in the trash.

Was I being totally wrong about Brad with his interfering in my life? I don't know, but I do know that I was tired of him thinking he was in control over me, and anyone that looked my way once I had gotten older. He never thought he had to protect me at any time when we were kids, but the way he's acting now was what concerned me. I really don't care for it or for him. I don't really care to see him ever again. I hated to be this way, family or not, but he has to understand he can't cross the line when it's my life, not his.

I had a rough few days at work after that, but things started to calm down by the end of the week. I was assigned two more teachers to work under, and they all wanted their copies made.... yesterday. They weren't very organized, and more often than not they ran late on everything they wanted done, which made me have to rush to get it to them on time. I was working under six teachers now, and their demands increased daily. Once they knew I was capable of doing what they wanted, they had taken full advantage of me doing everything for them.

I went to each of them telling them that I was overwhelmed with all their demands, and that I would need at least 24 hours advance notice of what they wanted from now on. It didn't make them happy, but I can only do so much at a time. They were the ones that had made the lesson plans, and they knew what they needed copied then. I could copy and laminate in the copy room the entire day, but they had to give me 24 hours heads up. The teachers could be so mean at times giving me the same nasty looks they gave to their students when they weren't happy with them. I was a nobody to them. They were the ones that held a degree, not me. I didn't care.

I thought about going out to the club that weekend, but had decided against it. I was glad I did. A huge fight had broken out with several people having to be hospitalized with severe injuries. One of Brad's old buddies from college started the fight, and had been arrested for it. But if he knew it was his old buddy, he probably wouldn't say anything about it. He had double standards for his friends, and for me.

I don't think I could ever explain to anyone who would understand how I felt about Matt. I know I was falling in love with him through his letters, texts, and phone calls. I felt so at ease talking with him, and I was so interested in what he had to say. I was counting down the time when I thought he should be done with his training, and really couldn't wait until I saw him again.

I think Matt might have been feeling the same as I

was about our relationship. He started signing his letters and text using the "love" word several weeks ago. I hope that it is how he truly felt because it would make things so complicated for me if I was reading something else into his closings.

Finally when he last talked to me he had told me how he felt, and I couldn't have been any happier than what I was already feeling. I had the biggest smile across my face with my heart thumping like crazy while we were on the phone. I didn't know if I should tell him I felt the same way until the pause in our conversation was too long, and he asked if he had out spoken himself. That was when I told him I felt the same way, but I was worried I would scare him off. My track record with guys wasn't the best according to Brad, but he assured me he wasn't scared off by any means. He was just glad I felt the same way. We couldn't get our words out fast enough when one was finished with a sentence the other had more to say. All I know is that I was the happiest person on the planet at that moment, and didn't want that feeling to leave.

After we were done talking I just held my phone in my hand trying to catch my breath. I was truly happy knowing that it was the real deal. I had to start thinking ahead into the future of the possibilities of what could come from our admitting our feelings for each other. I fell asleep that night with nothing but pure happiness in me.

With only a month of school left I knew I had to save as much money as possible to get me through the summer without a pay, other than house-sitting for Aunt Mary. I spent more money than I'd like the past few months, but all in all I didn't do that bad. The teachers had finally eased off on their demands since state testing had been completed, and they all are doing more fun things that they couldn't do throughout the year. That took a load off me. The last day of school was going to be a school wide water activities day. While the teachers were busy outside with their students playing in the water I had been busy packing up the rooms so we can all escape right after the kids leave. I was on my last room when the kids returned from the water day picking up their report cards, personal belongings, and left out the door. After several hugs from them they were gone, and I could finally leave myself.

It was a relief to walk home that day. The day was so clear, and with the sun beating down on my shoulders already I knew we were in for a hot summer. My biggest smile crossed my face when I knew I didn't have to worry about meeting the demands of the teachers for two and a half months. Two and a half months! But I also knew the days would fly by so fast that I will regret not going somewhere myself. Most of the staff was heading to Mickey's Bar and Grill to celebrate, but I had to get my stuff ready for my summer job at Aunt Mary's. I was just glad to be away from the school.

I had arrived at Aunt Mary's just before she had left, and put my stuff away in the room I always used while staying there. She lived in an old farm house that she had done some renovation on years ago. Kept some of the country charm in a few areas where other areas were never touched, and in my opinion, they should have been. One was the basement that was so dark and scary. I never liked going down there, and was glad when she had the laundry room moved to the ground level. Once she gave me her list of emergency numbers, a key to the house, and instructions on the what if's, she was out the door for the next two plus months. The place was mine now to keep clean, and to keep up with her list of chores she expected to be done daily. I always adjusted those lists after she left to a more practical schedule. It wasn't as if she would notice if the things were done or not. And I know for a fact that she doesn't clean the house like her list had stated for it to be done either!! I don't know who she thinks she was fooling with that! But I smiled, and wished her well when she left.

My first night there was loud with the rain pounding on the metal roof and against the sides of the house with the thunder and lightning that kept me awake most of the night. I never like those thunderstorms, and especially on the first night away from my apartment where I had only my stuff to worry about. I slept in longer the next morning a little longer than what I planned, but I needed that extra sleep.

I checked over the yard and nothing seemed out of place or damaged so I changed into my bikini, grabbed my cell phone, towel, sunscreen, blanket to lay on, and CD player to begin my summer tanning. I could go to the beach if I had wanted, but it was always crowded and noisy there. People and kids would run by kicking sand as they raced around. That sand somehow always found me, leaving me feeling gritty like sandpaper. I just went behind the old empty barn out back, spread my blanket out where I could relax, and tan as long as I wanted. The neighbor's corn field was several feet away from the barn so I was able to get as much sunlight as needed, and it was in an area no one would think of looking for me if someone came over. It felt like I had my own private tanning place.

I fell asleep that first day from the lack of sleep the night before which was a huge mistake on my part. I was sunburned, and it didn't feel good at all. I rolled over to get my back tanned where I again fell asleep, but not for as long as before, and didn't get sunburned as bad.

Once I was done for the day I gathered up my stuff, and headed to the house to shower off the sunscreen and sweat before starting my dinner. Aunt Mary had said that she had a ton of food ready for me to eat in the freezer. Just thaw, and put in the microwave were written on all the lids! She must not have thought I had a brain in my head to do that on my own. I definitely didn't needed to be told how to heat them in the microwave! Simple and time saving for me though. She wanted me to think she did all that special for me, but I knew they were all left overs from her parties, and when she grilled. She must think I couldn't see that, and have me believe that she had slaved over the stove preparing the meals special just for me.

Matt had called later that night asking how I was doing, and if I got settled in at my Aunt Mary's. I was glad to hear from him, and we talked for over an hour as I laid on my bed. Told him about falling asleep getting a bad sunburn earlier when he had asked if I had gone to the beach. I told him nope, just behind the old empty barn out back, and he chuckled.

Just talking with Matt sure made my day brighter. It won't be long until he's done with his training, and gets his next assignment. He will get two weeks of leave before he has to report there which he plans to come see me during that time. Brad and a few other guys were heading to the beach instead, and the married ones were going home to be with their families.

Matt didn't want to visit his family. They always brought him down because of his decision of going into the military. Matt couldn't see staying in his hometown any longer than he had to, and he definitely wouldn't go back there once he's out of the military to live either. He loved being in this little town in North Carolina the most, and would really like to live there if he could. He spent one summer there with a buddy years ago, and fell in love with the town, and its people. It gave him a sense of belonging. People there were just different as he told me. They were so friendly, and helpful towards one another. He needed that in his life.

I was counting down the days until Matt would be here, but to my utmost surprise, he had arrived earlier. I couldn't believe how good he looked when he was standing above me as I was tanning behind the barn. I had looked forward to his arrival for six long months.

Matt got on the blanket with me where he planted kisses all over me. He said I looked wonderful as he let out a wolf whistle. Matt had two weeks before he had to leave, and he knew I wouldn't like where he was going either….. Afghanistan. Matt was right, I didn't like that at all. Too many casualties have come out of that country. Knowing there was nothing he could do about it we had decided to make the best of the next two weeks, and try to not think anything about his assignment.

Matt didn't have a place to stay yet. All his buddies were scattered elsewhere, so I offered him one of the rooms at Aunt Mary's. No one would need to know he was there, and to be sure of that, his vehicle was parked in the garage, and I parked my car outside. He accepted the offer if I was sure nothing would happen to get me in hot water later.

When we got back to the house from having lunch at the cafe in town he brought in his duffle bag, and unpacked what he needed into the empty dresser drawers. The room was adjacent to mine. There were no hallways in the upstairs of this old house. To get to one bedroom you had to go through another one and so on. Farmhouses seemed to be designed that way to increase the room sizes I guess.

I sat on his bed while he unpacked. We talked more about our plans for the next two weeks. Once he was done unpacking he leaned over falling on top of me. I put my arms around his neck, and we kissed each other over and over. I had never done that before, but it sure felt good.

Abruptly he sat up saying he thought he heard a car door shut. I quickly got up to check, but there wasn't any in the driveway. I think it was his way of stopping things before we got carried away.

It made me wonder what he had in his head when we went to sleep that night, but everything was good. We told each other goodnight, and actually said we loved each other before he had kissed me goodnight. I laid in my bed thinking about him, and how I felt. I'm sure he was having a hard time sleeping as well because I could hear him toss and turn, and beat his pillow with his fist several times.

When I finally fell asleep all I did was dream, and even though most were good dreams I had a few that weren't good, and I would bolt up from them. I was glad that the sun was starting to rise because I didn't want to take a chance of that nightmare reoccurring if I had tried to sleep again. That happens to me often when I have nightmares like that.

I quietly got up, dressed, and made it to the kitchen without much noise. I started the coffee, and pulled out bacon and eggs to make for our breakfast from the refrigerator. Matt had woken up shortly, and was behind me once the bacon started sizzling with the aroma drifting through the house. He slid his arms around my waist while he nibbled on the back of my neck that sent shivers down my back.

I greeted him good morning, and gave him a little kiss when I turned around into his arms. His smile was dazzling, and he smelled so wonderful. I could tell he hadn't slept good from the dark circles under his eyes. Glad we had planned only to go to the beach that day thinking maybe he could relax a little there.

As soon as breakfast was done, and the dirty dishes were in the dishwasher we were ready for the beach. It wasn't as packed at the beach as we thought it would have been. We found a nice spot close to the waters edge where we put the blanket down claiming it our spot. We spent the afternoon tanning, and talking with a little swimming here and there. It was very relaxing. I felt he needed it after being in that school for six months, and driving as far has he had to get here.

That night we went to the cafe for dinner. When we went back to Aunt Mary's we turned the TV on, and tried watching a movie. We seemed to have ended up in each others arms kissing more than watching the movie.

I could feel my heart racing, and warm feelings stirring inside my body for him. He whispered that he loved me, and that was all it took. We ended up in bed that night making the most wonderful love I had ever known. He was the kindest most gentle man.

I fell asleep in his arms. When I woke up in the morning he was already gone. I was dumbfounded as to what had happened, and why he wasn't next to me. I put my robe on as I went downstairs noticing that his truck was gone from the garage, too. I rushed back upstairs checking the dresser, and saw his clothes were still there so he hadn't left completely. I started to get an uneasy feeling that sleeping with him might have been a big mistake.

I wondered what all Brad had told him about me by this time that Matt hadn't shared with me. I wondered what scheme was Brad up to now, and if he was the reason for my man missing in action from the house. I didn't have a past to be ashamed about, but Brad doesn't know or care about that. It wouldn't matter to Brad anyhow. He'd just make something up.

I went to the kitchen, and on the table there was a note for me with a rose from Aunt Mary's garden. He had to go into town, and would be back as soon as possible. He was thinking maybe we could go to the baseball game later, if I'd like to. I loved sports so that was a good idea. It would take us about an hour to get there so I showered while Matt was gone, and got myself ready.

By the time I was done showering and dressed Matt had returned, and kissed me good morning. He was very quiet on our ride to the stadium as if he had something on his mind, but wasn't willing to share it with me. Our seats were perfect, and we were enjoying the game with our team winning. It couldn't have been any better for us. Matt had chosen the best seats there, and he had popcorn ready for me to munch on once we settled in our spot. It was a perfect day with Matt. Matt knew me, knew what I liked, knew what I didn't like, and he did everything he could to make our day together great.

# North Carolina

❖

It was during the seventh inning stretch where the camera operators had gone around with their kiss cam. When I looked up on the huge display board in the middle of the end field, Matt and I had been spotted. Matt reached around for me, and we gave them a kiss that people would definitely remember. But, it didn't end there. Matt stood up while the camera operator had followed Matt's moves. Matt got down on one knee where he proposed marriage to me. I was shocked, and actually speechless by this. I looked at him, and started nodding my head up and down in a yes, like a bobble-head, before I could finally squeak out an audible yes. Everyone around us cheered as he placed the ring on my finger. I kissed him again and again after that. People congratulated us, and a few bought us a some drinks for the remaining of the game. Wow!! That was something I had never expected.

That was why Matt wasn't at the house that morning when I had woke up. He had gone to the jewelry store in town to purchase my engagement ring with high hopes that I would like it, and accept it. He had done a great job at picking it out, too. It wasn't anything super fancy, but I thought it was absolutely beautiful. He had taken me by complete surprise, and it was absolutely a total surprise.

Later driving home he had asked if I thought it was too soon with everything happening for us. I told him it was perfect timing. The timing, my ring, being with him….everything was perfect in my life. Matt wasn't the kind to wait on what he wants either. He goes for it right then and there with gusto. I asked when could we get married with his schedule as hectic as it was. Matt chuckled saying he thought we could go to city hall within the next few days to get married because he couldn't wait to make me his wife.

Within a few days? I didn't know what to say about it being that soon, and I was a little disheartened about just going to city hall. It was a cheap way of a wedding, if you could even call it that! Everything being done there is published in the paper, and at this time I really didn't want Bradley, my aunt, nor my mother to get wind of me being married. I suggested maybe go to another state like people do when they elope. I had heard of several places that would be much nicer than just plain city hall that wasn't far away. I really detested the thought of city hall completely, and Matt could tell that I wasn't keen on that idea. It definitely isn't the wedding I always dreamed about having. I didn't need a big wedding, but just not saying "I do" at city hall would work for me.

Matt mulled that idea over a few minutes agreeing that it would be better to go some place else to make it special, and said we would have to do it within the next few days because he would have to leave a day earlier to go back to his base to get everything completed for me, and get everything sent to my address from then on. It wouldn't be much, but Matt was insisting on having it done before he went overseas. That seemed very important to him.

Matt had explained that not only would we get money for living off base, but I would be able to sock away more money for our future while he was gone. All his banking accounts would have me added on, and his life insurance benefits would come to me if something would happen to him. I could continue to work at whatever I wanted knowing I wouldn't have to worry as much about money.

As I listened carefully as Matt was explaining all this to me, and I started to like the idea more and more. Eloping would also give me a day to find a nice white dress to wear, and Matt taking his dress uniform out of the duffle bag to hang in the closet so it wouldn't be so wrinkled.

That night in bed we talked more about military life, him being deployed so often for long periods of time, and moving from base to base when needed. That was when he told me he had a bad feeling about this up-coming deployment he would be going on. He said that he never had a feeling like this on any other assignment, but this one wasn't setting right with him. He couldn't put his finger on it as to why, but it was nagging at his most deepest and darkest thoughts within him.

That lead to another topic of what I would and should do if something like that should happen, and how he would want me to go on with my life. My eyes were filled with tears as he spoke about it which soon rolled down my cheeks. I didn't like talking about the 'what if's when all I wanted was for him to be safe while away, and to come back home to me when his deployment was over, but I let him tell me what I needed to know.

Home? That was another topic we had discussed. I didn't think I wanted to stay in my hometown any longer than necessary. That was when he brought up about this little town he liked so much in North Carolina. We decided to take a ride there for our elopement to see if it really would be a nice place to live like he thought it would be. We could do it all in three to four days if we both decided it would be a good idea.

When Matt was talking about that town we thought maybe we could get married there also. If it wasn't what I liked we could go elsewhere to get married, but it was worth the trip to see that town anyhow. At least it got Matt off the topic of his "what if's", for awhile. I wanted to stay positive while he was here, and that was such a downer for me.

It was late when we finally fell asleep that night. I had a hard time trying to sleep mulling over everything in my head that Matt had said. I must have been exhausted enough to finally sleep, but I knew it wasn't a solid sleep. I woke in the morning as if I hadn't slept any at all, and had a tremendous headache of a hangover-like feeling. I hadn't been drinking anything to cause it. But, I had things to do to get ready for our little get away, our elopement, so I had to try to shake it off, and get going.

On my drive into town later that morning I decided on going to the bridal shop first. Buying my dress/gown was the most important thing on my list that I needed to do. When I walked in, I was greeted by two gently aged women eager to sell me a gown of my dreams. When I explained I just wanted something simple, but yet elegant they knew there wouldn't be a big purchase from me, so they told me to take my time to look around. If I found something they could help me with that they'd be at the register. I had burst their little bubble of the money they thought they'd be making, but was glad to be on my own to look around. I was able to take my time, and looked carefully at everything. This was a very special time for me, and I wanted the perfect dress to fit the occasion.

Talk about getting a brush off from them after that, but there weren't many shops in town to find what I wanted. I looked at all the dresses, and at the many gowns they had to offer, but nothing was catching my eye. That wasn't until I saw a clearance sale rack stuffed in the back corner almost hidden away. My kind of shopping for everything else I ever bought my entire life, so I went to see if there was anything I would even consider. After flipping through several short dresses the gowns were next. I was so happy when I didn't have to go through the whole rack to find the one I really liked. I liked it even more when I saw it was in my size, and better yet when I saw the price tag. I pulled it off the rack asking if I could try it on.

The one lady took me to the changing room where I was able to try it on. Once I put the gown over my head

I gazed at myself from every angle looking at my reflection in those floor length mirrors smiling from ear to ear. It was perfect in every way. I felt very special in it. Even though it wasn't the gown I had always dreamed of I knew it was the one I wanted. I told the ladies it was the one I wanted, and they smiled as they placed it in a garment bag that couldn't be seen through. I'm sure they were disappointed it wasn't a high dollar gown, but it was every bit of one to me. They wished me well when I left. I was on cloud nine knowing I would be the bride dressed beautifully as I had always wanted for so many years. I couldn't wait for our elopement, and to a possible town I'd like to live in that was close to a base if needed. Life couldn't get much better for me.

The shoe store had several pairs of white heeled dress shoes for me to pick from, and I ended up with a pair I could use afterwards. They were really classy open toed with a strap around my ankle.

I shopped for a special nightgown for our wedding night while I was in another shop on Main Avenue. I didn't want to put much thought into finding a special sexy one because I knew I wouldn't be in it long, but wanted that as part of my dream since I was twelve years old as well. I felt rather embarrassed looking through them when I knew people were looking at me, but I didn't care. I bought one quickly, and left.

Matt had taken his truck to get it serviced to be sure everything would be good to go the distance without any problems. We met at the cafe for a late lunch. I was starved by then. Matt said the truck was ready for our trip, and on the way back to the house we stopped to get gas so we could leave early in the next morning.

Everything was coming together smoothly under the quick plans we had put together. Almost made it too true to be happening. Especially to me! Was it going too fast too soon? I thought about that several times knowing we wouldn't have many days together before he had to leave. Maybe we should wait until he came back home, but Matt wanted to be married before he left.

After lunch we went to the jewelry store where I bought Matt's wedding band. My engagement ring came with a band that Matt had at the house already. The one we picked out matched mine pretty close, and they had it in his size.

I had my small travel bag packed that night before we went to bed, and Matt had packed his duffle bag with plenty of clothes to last us a few days. My gown and his uniform would remain on the hangers to keep from wrinkling. The only thing I had left out were my toothbrush, hairbrush and make-up kit that I would need the following day.

Matt watched me from the doorway as I placed everything in my travel bag. When I saw him watching me he smiled walking in telling me how much he loved me, and how much he couldn't wait for us to be married. I was in his arms immediately as his lips found mine.

That night we talked for only a few minutes before falling asleep. I was so tired from the sleepless night I had the night before, and from the shopping I had done during the day so it didn't take me long after I closed my eyes to be asleep. Tomorrow was going to be a big day for us in more ways than one. I couldn't be happier with everything as it was right now. It was definitely exciting, and yet a little worrisome, too.

We were up early the next morning, and more than ready to get the day started. Right after we ate breakfast Matt had put everything on the backseat floor of his truck except for my gown, and his dress uniform. He laid them flat across the backseat. I quickly cleaned up our breakfast mess, and we were shortly on our way to North Carolina.

I had never been out of my state ever, and it was really amazing to see the different landscape from state to state. I wanted to see everything making the most of my wedding elopement. I didn't want to miss a thing. I wanted to remember every detail of the next few days. Matt and I had talked the entire way there on what we wanted in the future when he came back home, how many kids we wanted, how we wanted to raise the kids, to what we thought our dream home should have. It was such a pleasant ride, and before we knew it we were there.

Once we drove into that small North Carolina town Matt had talked so much about, I knew immediately why Matt had liked this place like he had. It was clean, the people were friendly, and as we drove around the square in the middle of the town, it was as if I had been there before. There was a flagpole right dab in the middle of the park surrounded by huge assortment of flowers, and a large white gazebo on the one quarter that also had various flowers planted along the bottom. Plenty of benches for sitting, and for people to chat with friends, or watch the kids on the playground.

The houses were on the older side of what I had expected them to be, but I knew that probably meant that the rooms were larger. The houses fit perfect in this little town. All the streets were lined with huge shade trees, and every yard was carefully manicured. There was pride shown in this town. It gave such a welcome feeling the minute we arrived that I had never seen or felt before. And then again, why would I have felt it before when I had never left my hometown.

We found the bed and breakfast we were going to stay at, and checked in. Mrs. Hunter was already at the desk waiting for our arrival. She not only ran the place, but she was the owner, cook, and housekeeper. The only thing she hired out was for was the yard work which she said she supervised with a wink of her eye.

Mrs. Hunter gave us the information we needed while staying there with Matt adding that we were also thinking of getting married as well. She then supplied us with the name of the Justice of The Peace, his phone number, and stated that he performs the services in the gazebo on the town square whenever he could. City Hall was across the square from the gazebo where we would need to get our marriage license. With that information, she gave us the bridal suite to stay in. We happened to be the only people staying there at that time, but then again it was the middle of the week.

We headed up the stairs finding our room at the very end. It was beautifully decorated with a wonderful cozy feeling. While we unpacked Matt thought maybe we should go over to City Hall to get our license right away before calling the Justice of The Peace, and setting up a time. I couldn't find my birth certificate which I knew we would need. I was frantic that I somehow had forgotten it until I finally remembered I had put it in the gown bag along with my shoes.

Matt had handled all the necessary paperwork needed, and made all the phone calls. By tomorrow at this time we will be married, and be husband and wife. Matt wanted to get a nap in before dinner so I told him I would be on the front porch when he woke up. I was too excited to take a nap. Matt had driven the entire trip there so I knew he was exhausted.

Mrs. Hunter was in one of the high backed rocking chairs when I went out on the front porch fanning herself. I asked if she mind if I joined her which she had insisted that I do. We chatted about the town and the people before I told her this was the town Matt had fallen in love with when he was here on a visit several months ago.

It wasn't long before she asked if we got our marriage license okay, and had called the JP. I told her we had our license, and that Matt had called the JP setting a time at noon tomorrow. I told her it was all happening so fast I hadn't had time to absorb everything like I had wanted to. I told her Matt was leaving in less than two weeks to go overseas. She completely understood. Told me she married her husband who was stationed at the nearby base after knowing him only a month, and never regretted doing it. They were married fifty-six wonderful years when he passed away, and she misses him to this day.

It was comforting to know she only knew her husband for such a short period of time before getting married because I was thinking that maybe we were going too fast, but on the other hand I felt like we had been together for a longer period of time through our phone calls, texts, and letters. I didn't want to make a mistake or have regrets later that I hadn't waited, but just talking with Mrs. Hunter eased my mind completely.

She told me where to go for my bouquet of flowers, and told me to tell Marge that she sent us there. Marge was her best friend, and would not only make sure my bouquet was beautiful, but also give us a military/friend discount. I told Matt about this when he woke up, and we went immediately to Marge's flower shop to place our order. Marge was so helpful picking out the flowers with me. I actually had a choice on what I wanted in my bouquet which I had appreciated because I had no clue what bouquets consisted of. Matt paid her, and she said she'd have it ready by eleven the next morning.

That night as we sat at the dining table with Mrs. Hunter we asked her if she would like to come to our wedding. Her face lit up, and happily accepted our offer stating she just loves to see young couples start their lives. She would be our only guest, but that didn't matter. It had made her happy.

Matt excused himself for a few minutes while he called Marge from the other room asking her to make a corsage for Mrs. Hunter in the same flowers as what we ordered earlier for my bouquet. Matt was always so thoughtful and kind like that. He didn't say anything to Mrs. Hunter when he came back to the table other than the meal was absolutely delicious, and he was stuffed. I know I was full as well, and we all agreed to wait a little while for the dessert.

Matt and I helped clear the dishes before we went for a walk around the neighborhood. I noticed there were many military families living there from the abundance of different license plates on the cars when they drove by.

Matt said the base was only ten miles away, and probably many families chose to live off base. The base was shared with the Air Force, and with the Army. Since the Air Force was there before they added the Army, they had left the name of it as an Air Force base. That was the base we would go to the day after our wedding to get me signed up for my ID card, and my name on everything else. This way Matt wouldn't have to leave a day earlier to go to his base to do it before being shipped out. I was glad I would have one more day with him before he had to leave.

I was eager to see what it was like on the base as well. It sounded as if it was a city within its own from what Matt had talked about. Things like a small church, commissary, stores, gas station, bowling alley, and hospital to name a few.

We went into the square to look at the gazebo we would be getting married in. Matt had squeezed my hand telling me it will be perfect. I knew it would be, too.

We sat on the bench watching people as we enjoyed an ice cream cone. I told Matt only a small cone for me so I wouldn't spoil the dessert Mrs. Hunter had waiting for us when we returned later. Many people that walked by stopped to say hello to us as we were sitting there hoping that we were having a pleasant evening.

When we arrived back at the bed and breakfast, Mrs. Hunter had warm homemade peach cobbler with vanilla ice cream for dessert, and joined us on the porch as we ate. She cut the pieces so large I didn't think I would be able to get it all down, but I managed.

The evening was so pleasant sitting on her porch and talking. A nice cool breeze helped the humid air feel better. After about an hour we said goodnight to Mrs. Hunter, and headed to our room. Falling asleep in Matt's arms was easy now as I felt that I was doing the right thing, and knew I was going to make Matt the best wife I could. I knew he was going to be a great husband. I knew that from the very beginning.

# Happily Married

---

I had woke up early the next morning to the birds chirping cheerfully outside our window. I thought that it was a good sign of what is to come for Matt and myself. The sun was getting ready to rise, and I could smell breakfast cooking in the kitchen.

Matt was still asleep so I carefully got up to take my shower down the hall in the bathroom. There weren't any other guests staying there at the time. I didn't have to worry about sharing shower time with anyone else, so I took my good ole time. By the time I was back in the room and dressed, Matt had woke up stretching his arms high in the air as he yawned. He saw me, and smiled asking if I was ready to become his beautiful wife today. I leaned in to him giving him a good morning kiss telling him that I was ready to do that yesterday. He pulled me down on the bed promising me that it was going to be a great day, and that we were going to have an absolutely great life together.

After breakfast we sat on the porch in the rockers making small talk about our future while drinking our coffee, and eating a homemade pastry. Matt was still worried about his future on this assignment though. I could see it was troubling him deeply. I knew I had to keep it on a positive level, especially today, because we were getting married in less than two hours, and I didn't want any bad thoughts to cloud our special day. He agreed saying that he was sorry he had given me the impression that he was unhappy. I told him I knew where his mind was, and that it would all work out for us. I just didn't want him to get cold feet today thinking he should hold off getting married until he came back home. He said there was no way for that, but last minute thoughts could change everything. He told me he would be at the gazebo eagerly waiting for me to arrive.

We had gone to the flower shop to pick up my bouquet, and the corsage for Mrs. Hunter. Marge had done a beautiful job on both. She was happy we were pleased with them. Matt gave her a big tip for doing it on such a short notice, but she wouldn't accept it. Told us it was her gift to us for our wedding which we thought was very kind of her.

I got ready in another room that Mrs. Hunter had opened up for me. Matt had changed into his military dress uniform quickly, and was already out the door to meet the JP early to finalize everything. Matt had told me as he talked through the door that he'll be waiting for me at the gazebo before he left. I had several minutes to spare. I decided to take a few flowers out of my bouquet placing them in my scooped up hair. It looked beautiful. When I slipped into my gown I looked at myself in the mirror. There seemed to be a glow radiating all around my reflection. A glow of happiness was the only way I could described it.

Mrs. Hunter knocked at the door to see if I was about ready to leave when I was putting my shoes on. I told her she could come in. She was all smiles when I handed her the corsage to wear. I was ready, and we were going to walk over to the square together to the gazebo where Matt would be waiting.

Once Matt saw me he stood up immediately. I knew he liked what he saw from the expression on his face. He met me at the bottom step of the gazebo where he hugged me. He whispered in my ear how absolutely beautiful I looked, and how happy he was for the first time in his entire life.

Mrs. Hunter was already up the stairs sitting in the chair provided by the JP by the time Matt and I turned around to start up those same steps. It was our special moment then.

As we walked toward the JP I had noticed several towns people had gathered close by the gazebo to watch us get married. My heart was filled with love from this town. We said our vows, and was pronounced husband and wife shortly. When Matt leaned in to kiss me I made it a kiss he wouldn't soon forget. Actually neither would I. I wanted our kiss to be the one Matt would always remember when we weren't together.

When we were done with our kiss there were so many people cheering for us with cars driving by honking their horns as we walked down the steps. Mrs.

Hunter had birdseed that she made sure she threw over us as she came over to congratulate us, and gave us a hug. Matt and I waved at everyone there thanking them as we walked back to Mrs. Hunter's bed and breakfast hand in hand. We took our time walking there basking on our wedding day as much as possible. I didn't want it to end!

Once we got to the bed and breakfast we had another surprise waiting for us. Mrs. Hunter had stayed up last night to bake and decorate a tiered wedding cake for us complete with a bride and soldier on the top. Marge and several people from the square came in through the door all excited for us, and wishing us well. Mrs. Hunter knew we didn't have family that would come from our talk the other night on her front porch so she made a few phone calls to her friends at her church, and they gladly gave us a beautiful reception. I was in tears with all the kindness from everyone, and especially from Mrs. Hunter. She sure was a gem.

Matt and I cut the cake and fed a piece to each other while someone had been taking pictures. I didn't know who that person was, and I could never catch them either to thank him or her for taking the time to do it. (Later I learned it was Mrs. Hunter's gardener who was also an amateur photographer.) He had been taking photos right along from the beginning to the end, and I never knew it. It was his gift to us, and his contribution to the reception.

After everyone was full with cake and coffee they had left so Matt and I could head upstairs to our room. I was in Matt's arms right after the door closed kissing him deeply. We may not have had family at our wedding that was blood related, but we had so many people that were like family to us now. Our wedding was very nice, and I couldn't wait for our honeymoon to begin.

The next morning after a late breakfast, Matt and I headed to the base to get me registered into their system, obtain an ID card that I would need for everything from that day on, and in the future. I had so much to learn about military life, and worried that I would mess things up. Matt assured me that I would be fine, and after awhile it would be second nature to me. Matt said everyone would be helpful on base if I ever got confused. I hope he's right because right then I was feeling overwhelmed with all the information that had been given to me already.

Everyone at the base were nice and helpful by telling us where we needed to go next, and who to see. While we were still on base Matt had taken me to the officer's club for lunch, and for a quick drive around the base showing me where things were located, explaining the areas that were off limits to civilian people, and why they were. I didn't think I would ever need to know all that information, but Matt thought I should know it regardless. I felt like I needed a map of that base if I was to find the places ever again! Within two hours we were driving back to Mrs. Hunter's place for one more night stay.

We sat on the porch in the rocking chairs holding hands while talking when Mrs. Hunter came out with tall glasses of iced tea asking if she could join us. We thanked her again for everything she had done making our wedding so wonderful. Her only reply was that everyone needs a little support in something now and then as if she knew from experience herself.

Dinner was delicious, and for the last time Matt and I took a walk around the neighborhood together. It was going to be hard to leave this town with all the wonderful people. Everyone was so nice and kind here, and willing to help out on everything they could. Something we would have expected from family. Family….maybe we had just adopted a huge family these past few days, or they had adopted us as part of theirs. It didn't matter, we were now connected.

Matt had fallen asleep earlier than myself so I quietly grabbed my robe, and went downstairs. The front door was open with a cool breeze blowing through the house. Mrs. Hunter was sitting in her rocking chair looking as if she was lost in thought. I didn't want to interrupt her, but as I turned to go back inside she had spotted me, and asked me to join her. She had an extra glass filled with ice, and a pitcher of iced tea on the little table as if she had expected me to come downstairs to join her at some time.

We talked on and on for hours. She told me about her late husband, and how he was always there helping her with everything like Matt was doing for me. She assured me that we were bound for a nice life together from her observations of us. I liked hearing her thoughts. It made things easier for me in my heart. I told her more things than what I had ever told my own mother, and it just felt normal. She chuckled saying that was so much like it had been with her and her mother, too. Her mom was always knocking down her friendships, criticizing her every move from how she ate, walked, and dressed. You would have thought we had the same mother with the similarities we have experienced. I confided in her that I knew my mother was going to blow her stack when she finds out I had eloped without her permission. We laughed together. I asked how she handled telling her mother the news.

Mrs. Hunter said that her mother was extremely angry at her, and had wanted to annul the marriage immediately. So her and Greg moved away during the night. It was several months before she contacted her mother again. Many phone calls were hang ups on both sides of the line until her mother had decided to accept her marriage to Greg. They became better friends then, and life was much nicer without all the shouting and name calling her mother threw at her in the past. I thought about the idea of moving away before telling my mother, but for the time being I had to finish the summer out by house sitting for Aunt Mary. If Matt's orders were to get changed suddenly I could always go there to live. Sounds even better now that I know Mrs. Hunter also had the same situations, and solved it by moving away.

When we were done talking for the night I had thanked her for listening to me, and for all her wonderful advice. That was then she asked me to please call her Helen from now on, and to please keep in touch with her. With that we hugged each other as we said our good nights. When I was going up the stairs I heard her locking the front door, and slowly walk to her own bedroom off the kitchen.

I didn't fall asleep right away. I was mulling over everything on our talk we had on the porch, and how everything was finally coming into light for me on what I would do for myself in my head. Satisfied with my plans I finally fell asleep shortly snuggled up against Matt's back which had woke him. He asked if everything was okay as he turned over taking me into his arms. I told him things couldn't be any better. I was very happy with everything, and with everyone. He kissed me good night, and I don't think my eyes were closed only for a few seconds before I was sound asleep myself.

It was hard saying good bye to everyone the next morning. Helen hugged both of us as she handed me a large Tupperware filled with her home baked cookies left over from our wedding, and extra cake. A snack to munch on as we drove home.

Matt and I talked all the way home. I told him about my talk with Helen the night before, and about the great advice she had given me. Matt was glad she had taken the time to talk with me. He knew I had some things on my mind earlier in the day, but was relieved it hadn't been second thoughts about being married to him.

Matt and I had discussed how we were going to handle our marriage news when people asked. I honestly didn't think anyone would even ask us because no one knew we were seeing each other before he would have to leave. But if it came up, it came up, and we would tell them we were married. Not wanting to hide it was good, but he also didn't know my mother like I did. I asked him to let me handle that one on my own which he had agreed that it might be better that way.

The next week we made the most of our time together. I was dreading the time when he would have to leave, and as hard as I tried putting the thought on the back burner of my mind it didn't work very well. I wanted to feel his arms around me every second we had, and love on him every second more. At night I would just watch him sleep taking in every detail of his face, hands, and body to burn it into my brain to last me forever.

We made some great memories during the remaining time Matt had left. Most of the time we didn't need to go anywhere, but several days we went to the beach basking in the sun. At night we would walk along the shore holding hands, and listen to the waves crash against the shore. I knew I didn't want the time to end when he would have to leave.

Our last night together was the hardest night making love with him. I didn't want it to end, and as hard as we tried to make it last longer we were exhausted. I had washed all his clothes earlier that day, and he packed everything he needed before we went to bed. He had a long drive ahead of him, and I knew he needed to get some sleep, but we thought just one more time making love would hold us over. And then one more time and again later in the night before we finally fell asleep.

We had breakfast at the cafe in town the next morning. I barely ate anything on my plate taking better than half of it home with me. It was the time that I was dreading as we kissed each other one last time before he pulled away. It was then that I let the tears fall, and I cried out loud not caring who saw or heard me. I loved Matt so much, and I was hurting bad already. I said a little pray right then for Matt to be safe, and to come home soon.

I slowly walked into the house as I wiped my eyes, and heard my phone ringing. It was Matt. He had stopped at the end of the road calling me to tell me he missed me already. I cried right over the phone telling him that I missed him, too. He got very quiet before he told me how much he loved me, and to be very careful before hanging up.

I held the phone against my heart for several minutes before putting it back on the table. I locked the house up, and just went to bed. I didn't want to remember this day any longer than I had to. I cried into my pillow. As I hugged Matt's pillow I could smell his body wash before I finally was able to fall asleep.

Matt's call woke me later that night, and I couldn't believe I had slept that long. He had arrived at his base, and was just letting me know he made it fine. We talked for several minutes before I knew he had to get his other stuff packed for his deployment. He would call me before he left on the plane in the morning. I blew him a kiss saying good night to my husband. I heard his voice crack as he told me the same thing. I knew he was having a difficult time himself.

Once again I tossed and turned most of the remaining night. Probably from all the sleep I had earlier, but none the less I was in no mood to get up in the morning. It seemed so strange being alone in Aunt Mary's house now. There was a deep sadness that crept into my head, so I turned on the radio while I did the dusting singing along at my hearts content. I also found a letter that Matt had written hidden under the pillow he had used.

I opened it immediately. It was full of all the memories we had made in the short amount of time we had together. He said he would treasure them, and for me to hold them close to my heart while he was gone until we could be together again. As I read his letter I could hear him telling me everything he wrote as if he was right there reading it to me.

This was going to be a hard year for both of us, and I was dreading it already.

# Unexpected Guest

The following week had to be the worse week of my married life. If anything could go wrong it went wrong, and I was feeling like a curse had been placed on me. The hot water heater quit working, garage door opener just hummed, garbage disposal died, the stove wouldn't turn on, the central air Aunt Mary had to have installed before anyone else beat her to it in the neighborhood, and last but not least, the refrigerator stopped working as well. After checking all the fuses in the breaker box I knew it was the appliances. I called my aunt's handyman letting him know of my situation with everything quitting all at once. He told me they were all very old, and were probably just worn out. He had suggested to Aunt Mary several times that she needed to update all her appliances, but Aunt Mary felt they could last her another ten or more years. She was very frugal, and didn't want to spend the money on replacing them.

He came over to check them all out. They were all pronounced dead shortly after his inspection. He offered to call Aunt Mary himself to let her know. I let him make that call because I knew she wouldn't yell at him like she would me, and if she did he would yell right back at her. She would probably think I had done something to them to make them quit working.

Later that day Aunt Mary called instructing me to order new appliances at the appliance store in town using her credit card she had in the top drawer of her dresser under the bunch of folded panties she never wore. She always thought no one would touch her old panties, so it was the perfect place to put things she didn't want to put anywhere else.

I was to then have her handyman install them once they were all delivered, and he could remove the old ones, and take to the dump himself. Three days of no showers, no cooking, or having ice, only from the small cooler I had brought in from the garage to keep some things cold, and I had decided to go to my place during the nights since I wasn't sure when the new appliances would arrive. I'd just have to go back to house sit during the day until the appliances were delivered. I didn't need to suffer myself until the appliances, and the hot water heater were replaced at her house, that was for sure! At least the handyman was able to get the air conditioner to run by replacing the condenser unit which had saved Aunt Mary several dollars. Her handyman was quite knowledgeable when it came to things like that. And on top of that, he knew how Aunt Mary could be when it came to spending the almighty buck. She probably was stingy with her money when it came to paying him, too for doing all the work he does for her.

On top of all that, I missed Matt to no end. I just wanted to cry, and crawl back in bed until everything was fixed. I couldn't deal with the set back even though it was only for a few days, and just prayed nothing else wouldn't break down while I was there. Heck, there wasn't anything I could think of that could break down that was left in that old house.

Matt called me the first day when everything had gone wrong. He could tell I was at wits end. I felt so much better after talking to him though. He had a way of making things better for me by just talking things over. I was the one who would get upset, and he was the one that could calm me down. We didn't get to talk too long because it was nighttime there, and he had an early shift in the morning. But what time we did talk made it all so much better.

I had finally learned how to use my laptop to where we could video chat on line. That made things so much nicer. I could see, and hear him as we talked. He looks really tired, and worn to the edge of complete exhaustion on some nights. Going to bed that night I thought how selfish I had been complaining about having a bad day until I saw Matt's face. I had been upset over the stupid appliances going out, and he was in a war overseas trying to stay alive. That made me feel like a jerk when all I did was complain on so many of our calls. I decided that was the last time he would see me, or hear me upset. He didn't need to hear my self pity when he had larger things to deal with himself.

Once the new appliances had finally been delivered

after three days of being delayed for one thing or another the handyman had everything up and running the same day. A few days later everything was back to being good at the house. I found several books to read in the meantime that Aunt Mary had in her library. After cleaning the place I would get absorbed in the story until I finished the book. It sure made the time go by faster. I had to admit, staying at her house wasn't a picnic though. I was so bored most of the time so the books really helped the days go by faster.

Going out back behind the barn to tan wasn't really a big deal to me anymore. I also didn't drive to the stores as often as I had at the beginning of my stay there. I had other things that I spent my time on. I called Helen several times when I knew she wouldn't be busy. We had developed a great friendship through the many calls to each other.

Aunt Mary had finally called to check that everything was working at the end of the week, and bragged to me about all the countries she had been to already, what she had seen, and how the men she had met had paid for everything. She was having the time of her life, and I was actually glad for her.

She had asked me if Brad had been by when he had his two weeks off before going overseas. I told her I heard he went to the beach with a bunch of the guys like I had told her earlier when she had asked, but I didn't tell her Matt had come to see me. Ha, came to see me, and us eloping! She didn't need to know that, not yet. That would be the kind of news I would tell her face to face when she came home.

I had wanted to think things through on how I was

going to tell her and my mother about being married. I thought maybe I'd take them out for dinner some night, and then drop the news to them there. It was hard to predict what they would say about it, but I can only assume that they would have a fit. At least in a public place they might not throw a tantrum as bad when they heard the news. It would be nice that maybe, just maybe, they'd both be happy for me.

I was buying groceries one day at the local grocery story, and ran into my mother there. She looked disgusting in her short skirt and a top that was showing anyone who wanted to look that she didn't have a bra on. It was so embarrassing seeing her dressed like that, and I knew the clerks at the register were whispering about her. Not only did she look disgusting, she was loud, obnoxious, and I could smell alcohol on her breath when she spoke.

She invited me to go out with her to a bar that night, but I had declined. She told me I needed to lighten up, and not be such a stick in the mud all the time. I would never find a guy holing myself up in my house the way I do. I needed to get out, have fun, be free, and maybe a guy would find me attractive enough for a one night stand. What?? I didn't need or want a one night stand. Never have, and would never would do that.

That was all I could take of her right then, and left her standing in the isle by herself. I could hear her yelling after me that all I needed was a man in my life to knock some sense into me. The cashiers were giggling when I rounded the corner as I quickly made my way through the door. I was so upset and embarrassed that I just needed to get away from her, and get away fast.

When I got out to my car I cried my eyes out. Her idea of finding a man was not what I ever had in my mind. I didn't **need** to find a man, I already **had** a man. A real honest to goodness man. One that was levels above her kind of men, and one that I loved, and who loved me. I was never going to be like my mother no matter how hard she tried to convert me.

I watched her stagger out of the store as I started my car pulling away before she could cause another scene with me, and drove back towards the house. I still needed to get groceries, but I was determined I wouldn't go back into that grocery store ever again. Those cashiers would surely recognize me, and I couldn't handle that. So I drove in the opposite direction from Aunt Mary's house until I came to another town with a grocery store. I made sure I bought a gallon of cherry vanilla ice cream to sulk my troubles in. I didn't think a quart would help me drown my sorrows this time so I bought a gallon.

Matt's phone calls weren't as frequent as they had been in the beginning, and I knew he was just exhausted, or out in the field. Either way I was worried about him, and was missing him greatly. I prayed for his safety every night when I went to bed, and for him to be home again soon. We always made the most from our conversations. Matt was always interested in what I had to say. We were missing each other so much that it actually hurt to get off the line with him.

It wasn't more than three weeks later I started getting sick to my stomach. Couldn't keep any of my breakfast down, and it felt as if I had the flu coming on. I ran to the grocery store once again to buy saltine crackers, and chicken noodle soup. That helped some, but it started happening again and again before I realized what could possibly be the problem.

I went to the clinic by that grocery store where it was confirmed what I was suspecting… I was pregnant. I just stared at the doctor when he gave me the news. I had left there with the paper in my hand that had the results on it. Matt and I had talked about having a family soon, but I didn't think it would be **this** soon. I still couldn't grasp the whole idea that I was pregnant. I was on birth control pills, and I made sure to never miss taking one so how could this be? I told the doctor what brand I was on, and he told me that the brand I was taking had been recalled because they weren't working effectively, and I probably should have been on a higher dose than what I had been taking anyhow. He had prescribed that lower dose to me just to be regulated my cycle, not necessarily to prevent pregnancy.

My head was spinning with that news. News I would have to tell Matt right away wondering what his reaction would be. I knew my reaction was total disbelief, and something I would have to accept, and prepare myself for. The doctor gave me a month's supply of prenatal vitamins to last until I found an OB/GYN doctor of my own choice that would take my military insurance. He said if anything happened between that time, he would see me if it was necessary. I was glad of that because I had no one I could think of that I would want to see about having a baby. I was in a daze when I left his office, and how I ever got back to Aunt Mary's house that day was beyond me, but I made it there.

Matt called later that night just as he was getting up to go have breakfast. He needed to talk to me before he went out into the field. I asked him all the usual things as I always did, and had told him I had been feeling sick the past few days. He asked if it was the flu. I told him not exactly the flu, but something else that would take me a few more months to get over.

He was puzzled until I held the paper up from the doctor where it stated I was pregnant. He looked up at me with the biggest smile forming on his face. I knew that he was happy with that news then. He also hadn't expected it to happen as quick as it did either, but none the less we were going to have a baby. We were going to be a family. He let out a war hoop that I was sure everyone there could hear. He kept saying he was going to be a daddy, and I was going to be a mommy, and we were going to be a family over and over as if he had to let it sink in as well.

Before he had to go he had promised me he was going to be the best father on earth for our baby. And a list of instructions to keep myself healthy and safe. He was sorry he wouldn't be here for me when I would deliver, but to know he would be there in spirit. I promised him I would, and when I hung the call up I had a sense of relief come over me that things were going to be good. I was relieved that Matt was happy about it.

I fell asleep that night thinking about becoming a mother, and I knew I wouldn't be the mother like the one I had. I knew that was for sure! Matt would make a great father. I had saltine crackers on my nightstand for the morning, but sometime during the night I woke up, and I ate all of them to settle my stomach once again. I sure hope this morning sickness wasn't going to last too long. I didn't like it one bit.

I had three more weeks left of house sitting, and was looking forward to going back to my own apartment with my own things in my own place. My mother had called, and immediately started in on me about not enjoying life like she thought I should. She sounded drunk already, and it was only two in the afternoon. Maybe I was too judgmental when it came to her, but she brought it on herself. She insisted I needed to get out of the house more, and to come with her that night to another one of her favorite bars. A friend she had there had a friend she wanted me to meet, and had been persistent that I come with her.

When I refused her temper had flared as usual, and she told me if I didn't come then maybe she should quit trying to help me find a man and then she hung the phone up on me. I sat there looking at the phone before putting it down. If she doesn't get her way she always throws a hissy fit. I didn't need for her to tell me what to do. For Pete's sake, I was twenty-three, and had done fine on my own for the past five years.

I was hurt and mad at the same time. I didn't need her to find me a man. I didn't need her to haul me to her bars. I could manage on my own, and I definitely didn't need booze or drugs to make me happy. She apparently did, but I didn't.

Later when Matt called I told him about what my mother had said. He thought it was a rotten thing to say, and it wasn't her place to find me male entertainment. He was so understanding when it came to how I was feeling, and in his soothing way he made the hurt go away. I agreed with him. A few minutes later Matt asked if I thought about moving closer to a base where I could have the baby, and not have to worry about what my mother or anyone else thought, said to me, or about me. I hadn't thought much of the idea at first, but the more Matt talked to me about it the more I was liking the whole concept of moving.

Once we got off the line I sat there with a pad of paper writing all the pro and cons on it of moving away. I had more listed on the pro side of the paper and quite frankly, nothing much on the con side listed that would mean anything of importance to me, or prevent me from leaving. I had to think hard on this as I have never been anywhere else, but this town my entire life. When Matt and I had gone to North Carolina that had been the first time I was more than a half hour away from my house. Moving to North Carolina would be a very good option for me, and I thought that would be my first choice. I would be close to the base hospital, and both Matt and I liked that town and the people very much. It was going to be a difficult decision for me, but one that I didn't need to decide on right away. I needed to weigh everything carefully.

When I set my pad of paper down I picked it back up immediately, and put it in my top dresser drawer out of the wandering eyes of my mother if she ever showed up for a visit. It was something I didn't need her to see, and have to explain anything. It was none of her business!

～

My decision had been made a few days later when my mother showed up at my aunt's house with two grungy men in tow carrying a brown bag which I could tell was a bottle of liquor immediately. She was pretty proud of herself when she waltzed in announcing that since I wouldn't go to the bar with her, that she brought the bar to me. I didn't like that thought of hers from the start, and I could tell she had already had a few too many drinks in her. She couldn't speak without slurring her words, and was hanging onto her friend, John, for support. Her dear friend was just as bad as she was, and what a complete mess he was. He needed a bath, a shave, and a haircut so bad, but maybe I was cynical because he was with her. Once they opened more drinks things got worse. My mother was hanging all over her friend, and his buddy wanted me to act the same with him. Ha, I don't think so!!

I had to push him away from me several times before the beans were spilled. He got angry telling me that my mother had told him I would be more than happy to sleep with him. He shouted this at me. I glazed my eyes at my mother who was so involved with her guy she couldn't be bothered to help me out. A parent is suppose to protect their children, not exploit them! What was the matter with her?

That creep kept trying with all his might to coax me into kissing him. Each time he came near me I'd move in the opposite direction. I kept pleading with my mom to tell this jerk to leave me alone, but she just laughed telling me relax, and to enjoy the night. No help from her was the worse thing she could have ever done. I needed her support to defend me, and to help me, but she didn't. She was in her own little world.

I finally shouted at her asking if that had been true what the other guy had been telling me. She gave me that snarky look only she could give while screaming for me to relax, and that it wouldn't hurt me any. I lost it then, and screamed for all of them to get out pointing at the door. I stomped my foot on the floor several times so they would know I meant business. They stopped briefly looking at me in disbelief before that jerk came towards me once again to get me in his arms. That was when I kneed him where it would hurt the most. He doubled over falling to the floor moaning with the pain I had inflicted, and cursing at me furiously.

My mother and her friend finally stopped groping each other long enough to yell at me that it wasn't very nice of me to do that when all he wanted was to get close to me, and to show me how to have a nice night. I screamed again for them to get out of the house, and stomping my foot harder on the floor this time as I pointed to the door. Why I stomped my foot when I did was beyond me. I think they knew I meant business then as they grabbed their bottle of booze, and finally walked out. John had to help their friend out of the house since he was having a difficult time trying to walk on his own. It served him right to receive that blow I gave him with my knee.

Just as my mother got to the door she turned around, and told me how much I had embarrassed her, and she would never see me again. I looked right at her, and told her as calm as I could that that was fine with me. I would never be a barfly like her as I slammed the door shut, and locked it as quickly as I could. I was shaking so hard, and close to tears. My heart was racing, and my breathing was fast. I had to calm down, and calm down quickly for myself, and for my baby. What a horrible scene that had been, and the nerve of my mother to think it would be fine to come over as they did, and bringing me a date. A drunken smelly sewer rat was what he reminded me of.

By the time Matt had called I was finally calm as I told him what had happened at the house. I could tell he was really upset with the whole scene that I described. When I told him I kneed that guy in his balls as hard as I could, he chuckled telling me, "atta girl", and asked if I was hurt by him. I assured him I was fine, and our baby was, too.

That was then that I told him I would be moving away from there as soon as I could. I had a few more weeks left house sitting, and then I would be gone. In between time I would get my apartment packed, reserve a moving truck, get the bank accounts taken care of, give my notice to the landlord, and to the School Board of Education of my vacancy. I couldn't take a chance of that happening again to me, and knowing my mom it probably would. She doesn't give up easily when she has her mind set on something.

Matt thought it was the best thing to do, and pleaded with me to keep all the doors locked both day and night, and when I had to go outside to be aware of everything, and everyone around me. I promised him that I would, and told him that I would keep him updated on everything. It was such a relief talking about it with Matt. He had such a way of making me feel better even when he was thousands of miles away. And we both knew there was nothing he could do to help me because of where he was. If he had been here at the time, I knew everything would have been worse.

Once we were done talking I called Helen to tell her

that I was moving there. I told her what had happened with my mother, and also the news of my pregnancy. She said she had a friend that owned rentals, and she thought he mentioned just the other day that he would have a two bedroom triplex unit available in less than a month because his renters were being stationed elsewhere. Helen said she'd give him a call right away, and see if I could rent it from him, if I liked it. I wouldn't have to worry about getting any references because she would vouch for me. I was sure Mr. Smitt would write me one as well if I asked, but if Helen was so sure I would get the unit that I wouldn't need to bother Mr. Smitt. Things were starting to come together on me moving, and it would go by fast if I didn't keep on top of everything.

I made a list of things that I needed to do right away so I could check them off as I got them done, and knew if I wanted to keep the moving date on schedule that I needed to start packing tomorrow. That led to a new list of things to do as soon as possible… packing what I wouldn't need or use for the next few weeks was at the top of the list.

The next morning I had gone to the store to purchase several boxes that I knew I would be able to carry myself, bubble wrap to go around the glass items, and several roles of packaging tape. Took them to my apartment, and saw the landlord giving him my notice. He was sad to hear I would be moving, but understood everything as well. (He knew my mother, and he definitely wasn't fond of her) He said he would help me with the heavy furniture, and knew he could get a few other guys to help as well. That was going to be a big help for me since I didn't think I should lift very heavy things, or try to go down the stairs keeping my balance being that I was pregnant.

I called the school board telling them I was moving out of state, and they appreciated me letting them know so they could open my position for others to apply. I went to the rental truck place to reserve a moving truck for a week beginning in two weeks, one way. I was checking some pretty good things off my list already, and it was only the first day of getting things started.

I grabbed a few groceries on my way home that night of fruit and items I needed to get me through the next two weeks at Aunt Mary's. I wanted to get home before it got dark outside. I didn't want to walk into a dark house after the situation I had with my mother and her two male friends. The first few nights after that had happened I heard all sorts of strange noises outside the house, and let my imagination get the best of me until I was up most of the night for nothing. Nothing but fear racing through my head that I had never felt before.

The other night I swore I could smell cigar smoke clear as day. I looked out my bedroom window to look around finding that there wasn't anything or anyone around to give off that kind of odor. I knew it wasn't my mind playing tricks on me. The odor was too strong to be my imagination, and I was wide awake smelling it. Several times I woke up thinking I had heard something outside my bedroom door, and actually got up to wedge a chair under the door knob so the door couldn't be opened from the other side. It gave me the creeps, and it got to where I could hardly sleep. Several times during the day I thought I could hear people talking, too. But I was alone in the house, or was I?

It was so scary staying there anymore. I heard things every night that I had never heard before in all the years I have house sat there, and I have been house sitting since I had turned sixteen. I knew it wasn't the TV or the radio left on by mistake either for the people talking noise that I heard. I knew something or someone was trying their best to scare me, and I had to admit that they had done a good job at it.

I finally had to go to my apartment during the day to take a nap so I could get some needed sleep, and to where I felt safe. I always made sure I was back at Aunt Mary's before dark checking all the doors and windows making sure they were all locked. I even went as far as checking all the closets, and under the beds to be sure that I was absolutely alone. Then watch a movie as late as I could before drifting off to sleep.

When Matt called the next morning before he went to bed I had told him what my day had consisted of, and he was pleased with everything I had accomplished already with my packing. I explained I needed to keep on a strict schedule if I was going to make it happen in the time frame I set for myself since I was doing this completely on my own. He agreed, and even offered me some other advice on packing that I hadn't even thought of, like marking the boxes to what room they needed to go to so I wouldn't have to dig through them to find what I wanted when I got to my new place. Made sense to me for sure. Didn't necessarily need to label what was in each box, but just the rooms would be a big help.

Helen had called me later that night saying she had talked to her friend about his rental. She said he would be more than happy to rent it to me since I was a friend of Helen's. Helen had put a deposit down for me right away which I told her I'd mail her a check in the morning, and thanked her so much. Helen said she was looking forward to me joining the community, and would help me with my move any way she could. Just getting me the unit apartment was such a big help, and a relief.

Helen gave me the address of the apartment, and the phone number to open an account at the bank over the phone. Her best friend, Lindy, was the one I needed to talk to since it would be over the phone. They usually want it done in person, but since Helen was one of Lindy's best friends, and a pillar of the community Helen didn't see any problem doing it over the phone.

Helen had the phone numbers for all the utilities I would need to switch to my name, and assured me it would be spotless when I got there. Sure was a big help for me, and I knew we were going to be long lasting friends as well.

Helen had taken photos of the apartment that afternoon, and sent me them in my email later that night. I was very pleased with the apartment, and already making plans where I would place my furniture that night as I laid in bed for hours before falling asleep. There was also a basement that had been completed that I could use as a family room or anything else I might want. The other units were larger, but I didn't need anything larger than the two bedroom unit. It was larger than what I have now so it was going to feel large to me anyhow. I was looking forward to my move more than ever, and decided I needed to get a few things packed the next day that I wouldn't need until I was moved.

I mailed Helen her check the following morning, and called Lindy to get that taken care of as well at the bank. I made sure I did all the communication calls while I was at my apartment. I didn't trust to make them at Aunt Mary's for some reason. All I needed was to go to my bank the following week, and have my funds transferred to that bank with my new account number. Also I had to call the base to have my address changed so everything, including my base housing allotment, would be sent to the new address. I also knew I needed to keep some money out for myself for the move, but not sure how much yet. I thought I'd ask Matt what amount he thought would be good until I was settled.

I had gone to my apartment that afternoon, and taped a box together. I started in the kitchen packing just about everything that would fit. I had three boxes packed, and I had only made a dent in my kitchen. I was going to need to come over as often as I could to pack if I wanted to keep on schedule.

I finally taped a few more boxes together before leaving that day. Grabbed a dinner from the cafe close to Aunt Mary's house, and hurried home. But I was shocked at what I saw when I drove down the road toward the house.

The sheriff and several deputies were at Aunt Mary's house. Their red and blue lights were still twirling around and around that lit the sky up like it was the Fourth of July. When I pulled in the driveway two officers had approached my car asking what I was doing there. I explained that I was house sitting for another week and a half for my aunt while she was on vacation.

He informed me that apparently someone had

broken in sometime ago, and they had caught him. They had him in the backseat of one of the patrol cars. The deputy had asked if I mind looking at him to see him if I might recognize him. He had told the sheriff that that I had invited him over for a few days, and that he had accidentally got locked out of the house. They checked the house, and there was a bed set up in the basement where he claimed he had been sleeping. I agreed to take a look, and my stomach turned over the minute I saw who it was. There sitting in the backseat coward down as far as he could wearing handcuffs was my mother's friend John. I knew for sure I was going to be sick, and stepped away from the patrol car just before I threw up.

I told the officer who it was, and that I didn't know his real name other than John from the night he came over with my mother, and another friend of theirs to the house. I told him what had happened that night, and how I had to scream to get them out of the house. I gave him my mother's phone number telling the sheriff she could help him with John's full name and address, but I didn't want to talk to her myself to get it. I had made it clear that I had not invited my mother over with this guy, or her other buddy for that matter. They had just showed up unannounced, and most definitely unwanted. I didn't want to have anything to do with them. When he read my mother's name he asked if I was her daughter. What could I say other than unfortunately that I was. He apparently knew her, and I had hoped he didn't think I was the same as my mother.

Apparently from the older officer, John had gained access through a basement window he had smashed through a few nights ago. The neighbor hadn't heard the glass break then, but when he broke another pane of glass earlier that night with the neighbors knowing I wasn't there, they had called the cops. I had heard noises the past several nights outside, and had blamed my imagination when it could have been him the entire time trying to find a way to get to me. Everything was starting to make sense now on what I was beginning to think was my imagination playing dirty tricks on me.

The officer told me that John had a story a mile long about me wanting to date him, that he was in love with me, and wanted to get in because we had a fight the other night, and he wanted to apologize for it. I starting shaking so hard, and shaking my head noooo stating it was all lies. I told the officer he was a friend of my mother's from one of the bars she went to a lot. I was **not** into that kind of stuff, and I definitely didn't want him there. Then, now, or ever!

They asked a few more questions before they left taking him to the police station where he would be booked for breaking and entering. I would be safe for the night with him in jail, but they did advise me not to stick around after he would be released.

The neighbor had blocked the broken windows with plywood already, but thought that I should think about going somewhere else until things blew over. I knew I definitely didn't want to stay there, that was for sure, and I didn't think things would just blow over on something like this! I thanked the sheriff and deputies as they left. I saw the neighbor walking over towards me with his wife, and waited to talk to them.

I thanked them for calling the cops, and for boarding up the basement windows. I was visibly shaking so they came in the house with me. The wife made me a cup of tea, and sat with me for a few minutes. I told her what had happened the other night, and that I didn't want anything to do with him, his friend, or even my mother.

Her husband checked the house over to be sure no one else was hiding in it. They had heard me a few nights ago screaming for my mother and her friends to get out, and knew they'd better keep an eye on the house after that. So glad they had. Who knows what I would have walked in to if they hadn't. I thanked them again locking the door behind them immediately when they left.

I was so furious at the whole situation, and especially at my mother for bringing them over there to begin with. I knew I wouldn't be safe now with everything that had happened. I quickly went to my room, and packed my things into my suitcase. I was out of there for the next several nights. I went back during the day to check on things, and put different lights on throughout the house using timers to give the illusion that someone was there, and called Aunt Mary to tell her what had happened.

She didn't seem too concerned about it, and when I was done telling her who it was, she asked why I didn't want him around. Had she thought that what had happened was acceptable?? I was shocked that came from her mouth. I told her he was a creep, a drunken jerk, and that I wasn't into that life style. She scuffed at me telling me I needed to lighten up a little, and live for once. That made me mad, and it hurt to think she was just like my mother. No concern for my safety at all. The last thing she said to me before hanging up was to contact the handyman to replace the glass, and to give the plywood back to those nosy neighbors. Not one question about how I was feeling, or if it had scared me. NOTHING!!!

I called her handyman immediately telling him about the windows without going into the details. Told him to come around noon the following day. I didn't want him to know the house was empty because I was not staying there another night.

I finally ate my dinner at my apartment later that night only to throw it up a few hours later. I was a nervous wreck, and couldn't sleep anymore. I got up and packed everything I could until I ran out of boxes. I was on a mission now, and the sooner I get out of this town the better off I will be.

# New Residence

I had assessed what I had left to pack yet at my apartment, and bought more boxes early in the morning before going to check on Aunt Mary's house, and to wait for the handyman to arrive. Everything seemed fine there, so I didn't stay any longer than what I needed to. The windows had been fixed, and he locked them for me before coming upstairs to leave.

I made sure I had all my stuff out this time. I was in such a hurry to get out of there last night that I might have missed something. I didn't have much there. Mostly my clothes, toothbrush, and such. I apparently found everything last night without thinking I had when I packed up as fast has I had done. Must have been my adrenaline kicking in.

I had made it back to my apartment in time for Matt's call, and told him what had happened. He was so upset knowing I was going through such a hard time, and said he had about all he could stand, and about it not being safe for me to stay there any longer. Not at my aunt's, not at my apartment, and not in this town.

Matt was glad I had gone back to my apartment where I had a much better chance at being safe. He was worried how all this turmoil could affect our baby. I promised I would get checked out in the morning to be sure everything was alright. I told him what my newest plans were, referring it to Plan B, and what all I had left to pack which wasn't much.

In two days I will get the moving truck, get it packed, and be on my way to North Carolina. Mr. Smitt had said he had a few guys lined up that would be able to get my furniture loaded in the truck for me, and would have it done in no time since I didn't have that much furniture to begin with. Most of it was the kitchen stuff, linens, clothes, and odds and ends which would be in boxes.

They were working longer hours at the base where Matt was, and guarding the place was getting more difficult to do, especially during the night. Many times their sleep had been interrupted with gun fire making it hard for him to fall back asleep very easily. The guys were getting on each others nerves, and snarky remarks were flinging from one guy to another. Brad had been the worse with his sarcasm, and his bullying to everyone. Many of the guys were steering clear of him as much as possible. He was not on any ones list of buddies to hang around with outside of their job because of his attitude. That had to have been bad if all the guys were feeling his rage and remarks unacceptable. They avoided him like he had the plague whenever they could, and went to their own make shift bar on the base for a beer without him.

Matt said that Brad had told him about the time when my mother tried to get me a date at his house, and how rude I had been to the guy. Of course we knew he had heard that from Aunt Mary, his mother, or even possibly my own mother if she was in contact with him. Matt acted like he didn't care, but was boiling mad deep inside. He wanted to punch Brad so bad, but knew it wouldn't do any good, and it would only get himself into trouble. Matt assured me that one of these times…. POW!!! He was going to let him have it no matter what.

When we got off the video chat I decided that I better try to get a little sleep. I knew I was tired, and knew that during the day no one would have the gull to come over or try anything with the landlord always there, and most neighbors were outside doing things in their yard.

I slept for a solid six hours which I must have needed. When I woke up it was close to dinner time, and I needed to get myself something to eat. I ordered a pizza and large salad having it delivered. I could eat off that for another day or two as well. I had plenty of milk, juice, tea, and water to drink, so I had no reason to go out. I didn't want to take the chance of running into my mother for any reason.

I packed as many boxes as I could making sure nothing would get broken in the move. I looked around my apartment at how bare it was looking. Rather sad when I thought about it. I really liked my apartment, but also knew when I got to North Carolina I would have everything set up again making it a home, our home. After watching a movie I went to bed thinking I would finish everything in the morning. There wasn't much left to do, but the sooner I got the moving truck the sooner I could carry the boxes down to it, and start packing it. Mr. Smitt was also going to help me with the car carrier, so I could haul my car behind the moving truck safely. I was really glad Matt had sold his truck before he went on his assignment. If it wasn't for Mr. Smitt's help, and the guys that were coming, I wouldn't know what to do on getting my furniture downstairs, and in the truck.

Moving day came, and my apartment was completely empty within three hours of all the furniture and boxes that were ready to be loaded. I ordered submarine sandwiches and Pepsi for lunch, and fed the guys helping since they refused to take any money. It was the least I could do for them, and they didn't turn that down. I poured Pepsi in their solo cups while they ate. They were so kind helping me, and they knew to pack everything carefully for me. Mr. Smitt was strict about that happening. I didn't want anything scratched if it could be helped. They placed moving blankets between everything before securing them to the side panels of the truck. I locked the truck, and went back upstairs when they were finished to a darn near completely empty apartment. Knowing one more box was all that I had left to pack was a relief. That was for the items I would need in the morning, and light enough that I could carry myself. I would put that box in the front with me along with my pillow and my sleeping bag.

My mother had called, and immediately started yelling at me for having her friend arrested the other day. I calmly told her that he hadn't been invited to the house, and I certainly didn't want him at the house. He was the one who broke in, and I besides, I wasn't the one who called the cops either. She was really mad spewing how ungrateful I was, and how she didn't need to see me again. I was about to hang up when I replied, "and yet you are the one calling me", which she didn't like one bit, and slammed the receiver down. I patted myself on the back for not shouting back at her. Matt had said to keep calm because that will irritate people more when they can't get into a shouting match. He was right, it worked!

Not the way I wanted to leave town with my mother upset with me, but there's no other way for me leave. I didn't want to tell her I was moving away, and have her show up on my doorsteps with her friends again, and possibly have the same situation happening there as it did at Aunt Mary's. Once was enough.

I could have my phone number changed, but she could always get it some how. I was sure. I guess she would have to learn the hard way that I wasn't like her, and never liked the way she was when she was drinking or smoking her pot. Tough love at its finest, but usually it was the parents doing it to their children.

Matt had called early in the morning to see if I was ready to leave, and how everything was going so far. I turned my laptop around so he could see I had everything, but one box, a sleeping bag, my pillow, and purse remaining in the apartment. I had to assure him I hadn't over done it, and the guys even carried down most of my boxes for me as well as all the furniture. He wished that he was there to help me make this move, and I did, too. I knew this would probably be my last time in this town because I felt I had nothing to come back for now. We talked a few more minutes before I saw his yawn, and told him to get some sleep. I would text him when I got to North Carolina. Wish I could kiss him goodnight, and fall asleep in his arms, but I couldn't, and even though it made me sad I knew it wouldn't be long until I could. We were almost on the downhill slope of his deployment. The last month before he comes home will probably drag on slowly, but I couldn't wait.

I rolled up my sleeping bag, and finished packing the last box before I made it downstairs to get some food, and to put the car on the carrier hooked up to the truck. I bought some extra stuff like apples and pears to munch on as I drove, and also bought a few extra bottles of water placing them in my little cooler with a few bottles of juice.

Back at the apartment my car was on the carrier in no time thanks to my landlord, and I was on my way. I looked forward to the drive, and getting there in about six to eight hours. By car it would take only about five to six hours, but I was driving this truck that was larger than I thought, and it made me nervous the first hundred miles or so. There weren't many miles that I could go on the freeway, and the county roads were busier than I thought they'd be for a Wednesday. I just kept my wits about everything, and started to get the hang of it like I had done it many times before.

I stopped about what I thought was the half way point at a rest area to stretch my legs, and go to the restroom. I sure had to use the bathroom more often now, but I was glad my morning sickness had subsided a great deal. I had packed a submarine sandwich for lunch that was left over from yesterday, and sat at the picnic table eating it with a solo cup filled with juice. I was so tired already, but only half way there, and I knew Helen would be expecting me later tonight sometime at my apartment. If I didn't show up she would worry herself sick.

I got back in the truck when I finished eating my sandwich, and was on my way once again. After another four and a half hours I finally pulled into my driveway. I drove straight in just grabbing my keys, clothes, sleeping bag and pillow. I was exhausted, and needed to sleep. I texted Matt to let him know I was at the new place safe and sound, but very tired. We made our texts short that night so I could get to bed, in the sleeping bag on the floor in the living room. I also let Helen know I made it there as well so she could get some sleep herself.

Morning came earlier than what I wanted, and Helen was at my door with some breakfast and tea for us. She thought I'd be tired from driving so she had waited until morning to come welcome me. It was about two hours later when she had a crew of guys from her church unload the truck of everything, and moved it into my new home. Helen had been over yesterday to wipe everything down for me so all I would have to do is unpack placing my things where I wanted them. My home was very clean, and I could smell the Pine Sol she had used.

I had bought several large pizza and drinks for the crew Helen had come over to help when they were done. All the boxes were in the right rooms marked, and I only had to put things away later that afternoon. They assembled my bed before they left so I knew I would get a good sleep tonight. Helen had insisted that they do that before they left, and they didn't seem to mind.

Helen followed me in her car when I returned the truck to the company so I would have a ride back home. We stopped at this little diner to have supper as my thanks for all the work she had done for me. She didn't have any guest at her place so she was able to have someone wait on her for a change. We talked for a long time after our meal was over. It was mostly about my move, my new place, my mother, and the horrible things that had happened to lead me to where I was then. She was appalled about my mother bringing the two guys and trying to push them on me like she had. Helen could not believe why anyone, let alone a mother would ever put their child in harms way as she had. She told me I was so fortunate it had ended as it did.

Once she dropped me off at my new home I was busy unpacking the linens so I could make my bed, and take a shower that night. Everything was easier unpacking than what it was packing. I flattened out the boxes when I emptied them stacking them in the corner to take to the dumpster in the morning. I called it quits early that night as it had been a long day. A very long and tiring day.

Matt and I texted for over an hour though. He was so disgusted with the base, and the other guys there. He said they were arguing with each other with the moral becoming a problem. He had to go outside to the area where they ate in order to talk to me without them wanting to know what was going on, and who he was talking to, etc. Brad was the worse. He told the guys about Matt thinking he was going to hook up with me when he was at his house before he was deployed, and how he had to set the record straight with him that I was off limits. I wasn't military wife material, and he just knew I wouldn't settle for him either. Matt just let the guys have their chuckle and didn't make any comments about anything that had happened. It was way below their ranks to be acting like they were when they were in harms way.

I told Matt maybe it was time to tell him we were married, and let him stew over that for awhile. Matt came close to it one day, and wasn't going to let Brad talk about us like that again. I'd love to see Brad's face when he was told though. More than likely Brad wouldn't believe him anyhow, but it would still be nice to see.

Next morning I was up early, and went to get a few groceries to tide me over for a few days. I was missing my fresh fruit in the mornings, and needed substance in my stomach to keep going.

When I got home I went through so many boxes unpacking them until my house was finally looking livable, and like a home. The neighbors came over that evening to welcome me to the neighborhood, and to the triplex. They were also military. Sadie was expecting a baby as well. She was a few months further along than me, and filled me in on the doctors at the base. Margaret already had two kids, and lived at the end unit of the triplex in the largest apartment. They both offered their services if I needed anything. I knew immediately we would become great fiends as time went on.

Helen came by with two high back rocking chairs for the porch as a house warming gift. I made a pitcher of iced tea, and took the tea out so we could sit in the new rockers and chat. It was so nice to relax, and feel safe for the first time in about two weeks.

Helen was still stewing at what had happened at my

aunt's house with my mother, John, and the other guy. I had never been told his name so I had no clue what to call him. I just referred to him as the knucklehead. I had a few other choice names I thought would fit him better, but it didn't matter. Not now. I was gone from there, and safe from all that drama.

Sadie and I became close friends fast. We both had something in common, our pregnancies, and were at home all day while her husband was working on base. Margaret had gone back to work shortly after having her second child. Sadie and I would see each other just about every day, and sit in the rocking chairs almost every night while drinking iced tea after she was through with dinner. It felt so nice to have a close friend like her, and for the first time in my life I felt like I could share things with her knowing it wouldn't be repeated.

She was having a little boy in about seven to eight more weeks, and was getting the one room ready for him. I took note of everything she had for her baby. Her mother and mother-in-law were always sending her boxes in the mail of things to help. She was thankful for that. Basically all she had to buy was the crib, changing table and a rocking chair for the baby's room. She had everything else she needed from them. How fortunate she was, and how wonderful it was to see both moms helping her out the way they were. Something I knew I would never have with my mother, but that was okay, too.

I took my laptop with me when I had my doctor appointments so Matt was included in the check up. He got to see the ultrasound at the same time I did, and how my belly was growing with our baby inside. I wished he was here to feel the movements I was starting to feel, and that we could do the baby's room together.

Autumn could be felt in the chilly mornings, and at night already. Sadie and I sat outside after dinner before the temperatures dropped too much enjoying the crisp air, and the colorful trees all around us while wearing heavy sweaters or sweatshirts. It was an artist display of the vibrant colors against the dark cloudy sky.

Halloween came and went pretty quickly. I passed out candy to the kids who came to my door trick or treating. I thought about our baby going out to do the same thing in a few more years. The future with our baby was beginning to be more prevalent as each week passed. I thought about all the holidays we would spend together when Matt got back from deployment, and just knew everything was going to be great.

My clothes weren't fitting me very good by then, and I had to finally switch to the maternity clothes. At least the fashion for them improved over the past few years, and the mothers-to-be didn't look like they were wearing a tent anymore. The clothes were more stylish, and I found them to be very comfortable. I found many outfits to purchase that would get me through until I delivered.

November was upon us with Thanksgiving right around the corner. Helen told me she always worked at the shelter serving dinners to those who came in for a hot Thanksgiving meal. I joined her, and it had felt so good to be helping others that didn't have a place to go. There were many people that came through the line that were extremely grateful for their meal. I thought of the many holidays I had spent by myself with a peanut butter and jelly sandwich while my mom was enjoying herself at the bar. I was never a priority for her.

Helen and I had stayed behind to help clean up after the doors were closed. It had been a long day, but a wonderful day of giving thanks for sure. This dinner for the less fortunate was made all from scratch with many people cooking the day before. They had a system down so I assumed they had done it several times in the past. The aroma was so enticing when you opened the door to enter. Once everyone had left, all the cooks and servers sat at the table to enjoy a meal ourselves. It was great being there with them, and I had that to be thankful for.

Matt had told me they had a great meal for the guys there, too, but he said it probably wasn't as good as the meal I had enjoyed. At least the guys were civil towards each other while they ate that day. Matt said a few guys took their trays back to their tent to eat in peace. Most likely the ones who were causing the problems all the time. And yes, Brad was one of them. Matt said he was the one who usually started all the arguments, and the guys had finally had enough of him, and his bullying. They complained to their officer in charge, who in turn called Brad into his office telling him he needed to knock it off. Brad needed to build the moral built back up before they have to go back out again because his group of men were sick and tired of his negativity, and him instigating fist fights. Matt wasn't sure what all had been reported on him, but when Brad went back in their tent afterwards he went right to bed without talking to anyone.

The next day everyone was busy getting things set up in the stores around town for the next holiday, Christmas. My favorite holiday of the year. Not so much about getting presents because growing up I only received one or two gifts if I was lucky, but it was the music, the colorful displays, the joyfulness from everyone, and the abundance of movies that always ended so nicely.

It wasn't until the last ultrasound I had that we found out we were having a baby boy. Matt was so excited over that news, and I was just as happy. It didn't matter to me what gender we would be having, but Matt was really hoping for a son. His wish had come true, and I was just happy that the baby was healthy.

I stopped over to tell Helen on the way home about having a baby boy. She was happy everything was going well for me, and our baby. She told me she thought I would have a boy from the way I was carrying him. She told me she was also planning to have a baby shower for me next month with the ladies from the church that we attend on Sundays, and my two neighbors if I was okay with that, which I was. She thought maybe in January would be a good time after the holidays were over, and everything had settled down.

When I went to tell Sadie and Gary my news, there wasn't anyone home. Not all night either. I knew Sadie was getting closer to her due date, but didn't think it was time yet. Sadie called me the next day from the hospital to tell me she had her baby, and they named him Samuel. I congratulated them telling her I couldn't wait to meet the little guy.

The day she came home I was over there pretty quick taking them a meal that they could eat later that night so Sadie or Gary wouldn't have to cook anything. Samuel was a doll. So tiny and precious. I held him for awhile until he fell asleep. Sadie put him in his crib, and we talked a few more minutes before I left. Sadie needed to rest as well, and I knew if I stayed she wouldn't rest.

Helen had every single lady invited from the church at my baby shower along with Sadie and Margaret. I couldn't tell you the love I was feeling from all of them. They were so very kind, and extremely generous with their gifts. From the looks of it, I will only have to buy a crib, and a changing table. I had been eyeing one in the baby section on base, and a changing table on top of a dresser that I was certain I would purchase soon. It was perfect, and it was duel use because after I didn't need the changing table, it came off leaving the dresser to be used.

Matt was amazed when I showed him all the things we had gotten for gifts. He said now we just have to get our baby born. March couldn't be here soon enough for him.

Later that night I bolted right up out of my sleep. Something was wrong, but it wasn't me or the baby. I got up to look through the house, and everything seemed fine there, but I had a horrible feeling none-the-less that just wouldn't go away. I had been shaken to the very core of my being with that sick feeling I was experiencing. I didn't know what it could be. I tried to fall back asleep, but had a difficult time doing that.

I couldn't shake that feeling all morning. I went to the baby store and purchased the crib and dresser with changing table top that I had wanted to get. I had several gift cards that I had used that almost covered the entire cost of both items. That was a pure blessing in itself. I couldn't wait to show Matt in the morning what our baby's room looked like when he called.

I assembled the crib later that afternoon, and got everything set up the way I wanted it to be in the room.

It was close to getting dark when I heard someone knocking at my door. Figuring it was Sadie I opened it quickly only to find two Army officers standing there with a sad look on both of their faces.

# Worse Day Ever

The officers at my door had asked if I was Katie Milton, and I nodded yes. What were these guys wanting to know who I was? How did they know my name? Why the heck were they here? A million questions had flashed through my brain in that short amount of time. The one officer had asked if they could please step inside.

I immediately knew then something had gone horribly wrong to Matt. Horribly horribly wrong! They had asked if they could please sit down with me. As I slowly sat down on the couch one officer informed me that my husband had been killed in action yesterday morning during a mission at an undisclosed location. My heart started pounding hard. I could hear it in my ears with his voice drowned out. My hands were shaking so hard as he told me that he was deeply sorry for my loss.

I couldn't move. I was frozen in my spot on the couch. I couldn't scream. I couldn't do anything, but stare at him as he continued to speak. His mouth was moving, with words coming out, but it was as if he was speaking to me in another language. This couldn't be true! I had just spoke with Matt yesterday morning before he had gone to bed. It was almost time for Matt to get in touch with me like we always had done. I stood up asking him if he was done, and asked for them to please leave. He wanted to wait a few minutes with me to answer any questions I might have. Questions? Right now? Hell no, I didn't have any questions. I just wanted him to leave, and to leave right now! I wanted them out of my house where I didn't have to look at them. They slowly got up walking towards the door with more apologies, and sympathy trailing behind as I closed my door.

I stood there just staring at the door until the tears couldn't be held back any longer. My Matt, gone? No way could that be true. We were going to have our baby boy in a few more weeks. Matt was going to be home this summer, and we were going to be a family. The family we had talked about having all the time. It couldn't be true. None of it could be true.

This was so wrong on every level. I had only spent just over two weeks with Matt through our whole togetherness. It wasn't fair at all. I wanted more time with him other than through a stupid computer thousands of miles away. Something wasn't right, they must have made a terrible mistake that it hadn't been my Matt that had been killed. Nothing was making any sense to me. NOTHING!!! I wanted to scream right then, but didn't have the strength to even get it out. My whole world had crashed that second the officer had opened his mouth. I was heartbroken.

The bearers of the bad news had been gone for only a few minutes when Sadie and Margaret were next to me consoling me the best they could. They were shocked, but nothing like what I was feeling at the moment. Sadie had phoned Helen as soon as she saw the car pull up in front of the house knowing what that had meant.

I had no idea that was something every spouse was well aware of when they saw a military car with two officers that stepped out of it, and walk to the door. Everyone but me. Matt hadn't told me that part.

Helen had arrived there immediately to be with me. I was a mess, and I was losing every ounce of life I had in me to try to understand what I had just been told. I didn't know what to think or say, so I just cried, and I cried long and hard. This was not fair to us, or to Matt's baby boy I was carrying. How would his son ever know what a great father he would have been. Matt had looked forward to taking him fishing, to ball games, playing football with him, and teaching him things only a father could do. That was all Matt had talked about since I told him we were having a baby boy. It was all gone now.

It was several hours before Sadie and Margaret had finally left, but Helen stayed there with me throughout the night. A night that I didn't want to sleep through. I wanted Matt to be okay. I waited for his call to come through at any moment, but it never came. Helen held me as I cried on and on. I saw the tears in her eyes as well. She was the only one that had the opportunity to meet Matt. She understood, I think.

The next day another person from the base had been

by to explain to me what I needed to know for the next few days. I had Helen be a part of the conversation as moral support, and to help me through what I was about to be told. My eyes were red, puffy and burning. I was still a mess. I didn't understand half of it, and quite frankly, I didn't want to hear any of it at all. I didn't want to deal with what had just happened. I wanted Matt there with me, not any of their words they were trying so hard to comfort me with were working. Matt had a bad feeling about this assignment right from the start, and he was right.

Matt's body would arrive at the base within a week, and I was to be there when they took his body off the plane. Helen had offered her assistance in taking me, and helping in any way she could. I nodded as I didn't want to handle any of this alone. Alone. I was truly alone now. No more phone calls, no more letters, no more texts.... no more "I love yous" from Matt. No more of any thing.....but memories.

The lady had handed me a letter Matt had written that I had taken from her hands. I couldn't read it right then. I wanted to do that in private.

Helen asked if there were any other casualties which the lady had said one other soldier named Sonny. I could barely talk with the lump that was lodged in my throat, but asked her if she knew if Matt had suffered any.

I couldn't remember that lady's name the moment she walked out my door, but she left me a list of things to prepare myself for, the times I needed to be at certain places, phone numbers, and a list of my benefits that I will receive, and when our baby is born that he too would receive.

Helen had made the arrangements for me saying she would help any way she could. She made an appointment with my OB/GYN doctor immediately to be sure our baby was okay from the shock I had just gone through. Helen also drove me to the clinic, and went in with me. The nurse got me in right away. The doctor said everything was fine with me and with our baby. The doctor gave me a list of support groups that were available to spouses that would help me manage my loss with any support or information I would be needing. He said that I would need that support. The people there were very loving and caring and that I should reach out to them as soon as possible if I was interested. He gave me his cell phone number in case I would need it should something happen. He spoke with Helen a few minutes afterwards at the doorway. I couldn't hear what he was telling her, but she nodded her head as she shook his hand before he left. I felt as if I was a zombie getting through that day. The nurses were looking at me so sadly as I walked out of the office. Or maybe it was because I looked a fright. I just kept thinking of Matt.

I watched as the plane with Matt's body on had arrived at the base wondering what could have happened. I didn't know anything except thinking of how and why, and wondered what his last thoughts might have been. I felt so sad. Then I would start to get angry. Why???? This just could not be happening. As I stood there watching everything going on I couldn't help but wonder if Sonny's family was going through the same things as I was right now. My heart ached for them as well. I remembered the name Sonny from Matt talking about the guys, and Matt thinking that Sonny was a good guy in his book. A family man with two young children.

The slow departure from the plane was very somber once the plane had landed, and had the engines turned off. The back ramp opened up. Ever so slowly the men were taking a step at a time down the ramp carrying Matt's body in a casket that had been draped with the American flag. They stopped in front of me to give me their condolences, and saluted Matt's body one last time before they placed his casket in the hearse to transport him to the funeral home. There was also a soldier at Matt's side from the time he left for home that would stay with him until Matt was laid to rest. I didn't know why at that time either.

Helen and I had followed the hearse to the funeral home in her car where I met with the director. I didn't have anyone other than Helen, and my neighbors to hold a large service, but the director had insisted on putting Matt in their largest room available being that this community was a strong supportive one, especially for the military families. A plot at the cemetery had been chosen that day as well.

The minister from the church Helen and I attended had walked in offering his condolences, and to discuss the services for Matt's funeral with me. Helen had called him the night before to arrange for him to be there when she came to my house, but I had fallen asleep. He had told Helen he'd have to meet with us today, and have my permission directly. He was so kind, but his soothing words he tried to say fell deaf on my ears. He tried telling me that we all have a path of light in our lives, and only a certain amount of time for living each day. It had been Matt's time to leave. I had never thought that Matt would be called to the heavens so soon. I didn't want to hear anymore of his sermon to me. I knew he was trying to be kind to help me understand, but it wasn't helping me. I just nodded, and watched everything going on around me in a complete blur. I was numb to everyone, and to everything happening.

I didn't want the day to come when I would have to give Matt my final farewell. I slowly dressed in Matt's favorite dress as tight as it felt across my belly, and drank a glass of juice when I had finished. I knew I wouldn't be able to hold food down so juice was it for now. I needed something in my stomach, and some kind of nourishment for our baby.

The funeral home sent their limousine to pick me up at the time I had requested. I had wanted it to arrive early, because I had wanted some private time to see Matt before Helen and the minister arrived. Sadie and Margaret said they would be at Matt's service with their husbands as well.

When I went into the funeral home, Mr. Holmes had greeted me at the door, and ushered me to the room where they had Matt's casket set for the service. He quietly excused himself to give me the privacy I needed. Matt's escort was standing there also who told me to take whatever time I needed, and moved just out of sight in case I needed him. I walked ever so slowly to the casket to see Matt, and burst into uncontrollable tears. Matt looked so handsome in his uniform. He looked like he was just laying there asleep. I talked to Matt so softly getting everything out that I needed to tell him. I reached for his hand to hold, and held it against my belly telling Matt our son would know he had a wonderful daddy that loved him so very much even before he was born, and all the wonderful things about him. I placed his hand back inside on his chest. I finally kissed my fingers placing them on Matt's lips telling him until we meet again, how much I would miss him, and that I would always love him.

I heard someone walk in behind me. I turned around to see that it was Helen and our minister walking towards me. I was a mess, and couldn't stop crying. Helen hugged me tightly as she guided me to my seat. Helen brought a whole box of tissue with her as she knew I would need plenty to get me through this.

Sadie and Margaret with their husbands walked in next, and then more and more people started walking in. Many were from the base because they were in uniform, and several people were from our church as well. Before I knew it the entire room was filled, and the funeral director had to open another room by sliding the partition to the side.

It looked as if the entire town had been there for Matt, and it was so overwhelming for me. They all followed us to the cemetery where Matt would lay in peace for eternity after the service. After the twenty-one gun salute had been done, which had startled me each time they shot off their rifles, and after that the Taps were played they presented me with the American flag now folded that had been draped over Matt's casket. The service was so beautiful. Matt deserved it, and thanks to Helen and this town, he received it. The minister interrupted everyone's chatter by inviting everyone to the church fellowship hall afterwards for a lunch provided by the ladies of the church.

I had not expected this as I had planned to just go home. The church ladies out did themselves. There was enough food there to feed an entire troop of Army personnel. Army! The very thing Matt was so proud to be a part of. Every single person there came up to me to tell me how sorry they were for my loss, and our baby's loss. They were heartfelt messages that meant a lot for me to hear. I didn't think I needed to hear anything, but I did, and I had appreciated each and every thing everyone had said. So many knew Matt from the military, and had told me he was a great guy. I already knew that myself, but I thanked everyone for their kind words.

I was totally drained when I finally got back home that night. I went straight to bed where I fell into a deep sleep. Matt came to me in my dreams that night telling me everything would be alright, and he knew our baby was a blessing to both of us. He kissed my forehead before leaving. My dream had felt so real. It was so comforting to know Matt had came to me, even if it had been in a dream. I hope Matt continues to come to me so I won't feel so alone. I was alone without Matt next to me in bed whispering his "I Love You's" to me the way he always did. Oh Matt…….

I was alone, and I wasn't sure how I would be able to go on without him. Death was permanent. No do-overs or try better the next day because there wasn't going to be another day. Matt's life was over, and it sucked. I stayed in bed for days only getting up for food, and that was only for the baby's sake that I had done that. Helen called checking on me daily until I asked her not to call as often. I needed to grieve in my own way, and my way was to be left alone a while to do so. She understood, and told me to call her when I was feeling better. I did the same with Sadie and Margarite.

It wasn't until I had smelled my pillow where the oils from my hair had made a disgusting odor that I finally got up, took a shower, and changed the sheets on my bed. One look in the mirror, and it was obvious that I wasn't well. I thought of all the people that have, and still were reaching out to me to help in any way that they could, or that I needed. That was when I realized that I wasn't alone. I had Helen, Sadie, and Margarite right by me, and all the women in the church that had been so kind. I decided right then I needed to think more of myself than a weakling like Brad had called me when we were kids. Yes, I was weak, and maybe Brad had been right. Maybe I wasn't cut out to be a military wife. Well, I will show him how wrong he was, and I will grab my situation by the horns, and trudge on the best way I could. I had to do this for myself, for Matt, and for our baby.

A few more days had passed before I finally had the courage to read my letter from Matt. I cried through most of it, but it was the most sweetest letter for a farewell letter. I could hear Matt talking as I was reading it, and his voice was soothing. When I was done I held it to my heart promising to raise our son with all his love as well. That was all I could do at this point.

I sat at the edge of our bed thinking how we had been short changed on our married life together. I thought about everything we had done in the short amount of time we had. I had saved all of our video chat calls, and would save them forever. I wanted our son to see him, and hear of the wonderful things Matt had to say. Especially how excited he was knowing we were going to have a baby boy. His baby boy.

I sat in my rocking chair on the front porch one night thinking about all the wonderful times Matt and I had together in that short amount of time. I wouldn't trade it for the world either. We never had a harsh word between us, probably because we were only together for a short time, but none-the-less. Matt was the perfect husband in all respects that anyone could have asked for. I was the lucky one he had chosen to be his wife. My heart ached for him not being there with me. I knew I would have to take charge of everything in my life by myself now, and I was determined that I would make Matt proud. I had to. I was all that he had for family.

I had made sure that Matt's family had been notified of his services, but I didn't see any of them that I was aware of. I had never met them, but from what Matt had told me, I would have recognized them immediately. I found that to be sad that they didn't come, but like Matt had told me that they were never a part of his life. He had sent them money from time to time until he heard they didn't make good use of it. It mostly had gone towards their beer, cigarettes, and drugs. That was when he decided he wasn't going to support their bad habits any longer. He might as well have ripped his money up, and thrown it out of a window. He tried to pay a few of their bills, but some how or another they were able to get their hands on that money as well. It was a losing situation for him so he quit sending them anything. They never even wrote him a single letter while he was gone.

Matt had warned me about them if they would happen to come around. They would steal things from other people to pawn off for money, and he didn't want that to happen to me. Not that we had anything of great value, but that didn't matter to them. I never expected them to show up at our house, but it was something I needed to keep myself aware of just in case they had.

All the personal things that Matt had overseas with him were brought to me right away. I had set everything on the table in the kitchen without ever looking in the box. Once I did look through that box, and thought how sad that his whole life was held in that one cardboard box. It was nicely packed, and on top of his belongings was a letter written to me from his base commander. In the letter he had written he had stated what a great guy Matt was to the troops, and Matt had told him so much about me, and about how much Matt loved me. Matt was very proud of me, and excited about becoming a father in the near future. The letter had gone on and on about Matt that was so nice to hear. Matt had done a great job because that was the person he was. Matt had never backed down from any assignment he had been assigned to, and gave it his all. He was going to be missed by many. I thought to myself that he wasn't going to be missed by them as much as I was missing him.

As I continued looking through his things, I found several pictures taken of him at that base. Someone had placed them in the box for me to have. Matt had several pictures of me glued on his laptop that I had sent him, and more in his wallet where he had drawn hearts all around them. There was a box I hadn't recognized by Matt's wallet. I opened it, and there was a Purple Heart medal that had been addressed to me. Matt's Purple Heart for being injured in action. Injured and killed. I quickly put everything back in that box, and placed it in our bedroom closet on the top shelf. I did keep out the pictures of Matt setting them on my nightstand so I could look at them whenever I wanted.

# It's Time!

I somehow managed to get through the following weeks accepting the simple yet complicated fact that I was really on my own now for everything other than friends helping me when needed. It hadn't been easy to adjust to that fact by any means, and I wondered if I would ever be able to adjust completely. Matt had been my everything since the day we had met. My rock, my best friend, my support when things weren't going good for me, and a cheerleader when things were going great. Like I said, my everything. Matt had a way of talking me through every situation with his soothing voice that calmed me down a good number of times. Oh, how I wish he was here now. Every minute of the day I had thought about Matt no matter where I was, or what I would be doing at the time. Even a simple song that would come on the radio, and I would think of the last time I had heard it with Matt. Matt had made such a big impact on me, and my life in that short amount of time that we had together. I had been blessed with such a wonderful guy that I can't believe this had happened to him. That is until I look down at my protruding belly!

Sadie, Margaret, and Helen were such dear friends to me, but it wasn't the same as it was with Matt. I didn't want to burden them with any of my problems, but I knew they were always there to listen to me if needed. Helen made sure I was okay for weeks after Matt's death by either stopping by, or calling me. Many times she'd bring something yummy with her that she had baked earlier in the day, and we'd eat it while enjoying our coffee as we chatted. All my friends were trying their best to comfort me in one way or another.

Of all times for my mother to call was that one day that I was a little emotional over everything. I almost didn't answer the phone, but after six times ringing I thought it might have been something important, and maybe, just maybe she was in a good mood to listen to me for once. But it wasn't that way. She wanted to tell me she was getting married, again. Her wonderful John had proposed last week which she had accepted, and was thrilled to death about. She wanted me to attend her wedding. It was going to be held at the park in town because they were short on funds at the moment. How could two grown adults come up short all the time was beyond me. She had hinted around that she could use some extra money to help with the expenses, but I played dumb to it because I knew she would use it to buy more liquor. Not after the last time she had asked me for money, and had done exactly that. I had explained that

I'm on a tight budget myself so she would need to get money from some other person or source.

I had to think about how many weddings I had attended of hers? I think this one would make number five…. maybe six, and I didn't feel she'd miss me at this one. I had been to all the others, and most of those marriages didn't make it past the two year anniversary before she had found fault about her husband over one thing or another, and filed for divorce. It was also during the week that I was due to deliver my baby which was more important to me. She threw a fit when I told her that I couldn't be there. Apparently she didn't realize I didn't live in that town anymore either. Before I had a chance to tell her that I was having a baby around that time she had slammed the phone in my ear once again. I really didn't need to hear from her that day. I had tried to keep things positive, but when she flies off the handle like she often does, I always have a hard time dealing with it later. I often wonder if her drinking was the cause of her irrational behavior when it came to me, or if there another issue involved.

When I went in for my latest check-up, which I had to do weekly now. The doctor told me to keep doing what I have been. Our baby was slowly getting into position, and in a few weeks or so he would be ready to be born. The doctor had asked how things have been for me, and if I had anyone to help me after the baby was born. All I could think of was Helen and Sadie. I knew Helen would be there regardless. When I went outside I rubbed my belly telling my baby to hang in there a little longer. I looked up at the clouds whispering to Matt that we were doing fine, and how much we loved and missed him before getting in the car to drive home.

The weather had been so cold lately that I went out as little as possible. I didn't trust my driving in bad weather on the roads, and it was difficult for me trying to manage the steering wheel with my belly in the way. It was a tight squeeze for me, and I didn't feel it was good for the baby to be pushed tightly against the steering wheel as he was.

I had decided to visit Helen for awhile since I hadn't been there for some time before heading home that day. She invited me to stay for lunch. We sat at the kitchen table talking for most of the afternoon with me telling her what the doctor had asked about anyone I could rely on when I'm ready to deliver. I needed someone I could get a hold of easily to take me to the hospital. I smiled at Helen as she reached over the table to squeeze my hand as she said she would be there for me for anything, and everything. I knew I could count on her. I thanked her for everything before leaving.

I had made it home just before dark. I never liked going into any of my places after dark. Particularly when I hadn't left a light on inside, and especially after that incident at my Aunt Mary's house that time. Matt had asked me to to be super careful, and always be aware of my surroundings when I came or went anywhere from the house.

I grabbed a book I had been reading, and curled up on the couch as I read a few more chapters before the news came on, and the movie I planned to watch afterwards. My days were long, but my nights were the worse. It had been really the worse when the seasonal time had changed, and it was dark by six. It didn't feel as if the nights would ever end.

I couldn't shut my brain off when I went to bed thinking either. Always thinking of everything I needed to do yet, things I should be doing, things I wish I could change, and so on and so on. I knew it wouldn't be safe for the baby if I took something to help with the sleep either. Many nights I would get back up to drink a cup of hot sleepy time tea, or drink a glass of milk while flipping the TV on. It didn't take too long to get tired then. Probably because I was past tired, and near exhaustion by the time I did fall asleep. Many times I woke up on the couch where I had been the night before with the TV still on.

I would visit with Sadie during the day. We hadn't had much time to talk since Sammy had been born. Sadie was so busy with him, keeping the house clean, and doing what she needed to do for Gary. I needed to know how she was doing it during the day with their baby. She had help right from the beginning from her family after Sammy was born to get her ready for when she would be there alone. I wasn't expecting Helen to stay two weeks with me. I thought just a day or two until I was rested enough to take over would be enough.

My weekly appointments were going fine, but I was getting very uncomfortable more and more each day. My thoughts about Matt were nonstop wishing he was still with us. I knew it wasn't doing me any good doing that to myself, but for me it made me feel better thinking of him. We had some wonderful times together, and I loved him with all my heart. When I thought about Matt more often than not our baby would give me a good kick in the ribs as if he agreed with me.

One night late a pain hit me that woke me up from my sleep. I rolled over to my other side, and it hit again. That time I sat up to look at the clock before I laid back down. Then another pain. I knew it wasn't the baby kicking me any longer. I was in early labor, and I needed to make preparations to get to the hospital. The pains kept getting closer and longer each time. I finally called Helen to tell her it was time. She made it to my place in less than five minutes. With no one on the streets I'm sure Helen had put the pedal to the metal forgetting there were stop signs along the way.

I was waiting at the door when Helen pulled in the driveway, and slowly walked out to her car between contractions. Just before I went to get in the car my water had broke, and I was soaked. Helen jumped out of the car to help me finish getting in. She had several towels in the back she had placed on the seat for me to sit on. By the time we got to the hospital the pains were constant. The nurses had ushered me into the room for me to change into one of their hospital gowns, and for them to check to see how far along I had dilated. I was definitely far enough for the doctor to be called.

About that time the doctor had walked in the delivery room asking if I was ready to bring my baby into the world. I was ready to deliver, and I knew my baby wasn't going to wait any longer. No sooner was I situated on the delivery table the doctor had told me he was ready, and on the next contraction I was to push. I felt the contraction starting, and gave a good solid push. Before I knew it I didn't feel anymore pressure, and I had heard a little cry. I had delivered my baby. They nurses wiped him down a little before handing him to me.

I couldn't believe how much he looked like Matt, and as the doctor finished his work on me I was enjoying my baby. I planted several kisses on him while I cried thanking God he was so perfect. Ten fingers, ten toes, beautiful coloring, and a load of dark curly hair on his head just like Matt had. The nurse had to take him to another room to weigh him, put a band on his tiny foot, take a footprint, and blood drawn from his little heel. I couldn't wait for her to bring him back to me.

I held him as they took me to my room where Helen had been waiting for us. She stood up with a big smile on her face as she held him telling me he was the mini version of Matt for sure. Such a beautiful baby. They brought a newborn crib into my room so I would have him there all the time with me, and a nurse checking in every half hour or so to help me if I needed it. I was bedridden so the nurse would get my baby for me for feeding, and return him to the crib when I was done.

Helen had stayed for about an hour before having to leave. It was starting to break dawn, and she had a few guests at her bed and breakfast that she needed to prepare breakfast for. She had to have been exhausted from helping me, but I'm sure her guests would understand when she told them the news. I thanked her for getting me to the hospital in time to deliver our baby. She smiled saying she would have been hurt to miss out on this special occasion.

I slept soundly for a few hours until the baby woke me wanting to be fed, and probably a diaper change as well. The nurse was right there getting him with one arm, and a bottle of formula in the other to bring over to me. Baby was making such a fuss, but as soon as he was in my arms he would settled down quickly. Probably because I was feeding him, but none-the-less he had settled down. After a few burps I held him for awhile finding it hard to believe I had just had this baby, this tiny little human I was holding in my arms. I was now a mother, and I was going to raise him the best I could the way Matt and I had planned.

Before I left to go home I had to name him for his birth certificate. I had no other name in mind, but to name him after his father. Matt and I had talked about other names, but I wanted Matthew Jerome Milton II, and under the circumstances it was appropriate, so that is what I went with.

Helen showed up to drive us home, and help me get settled in my house before she left me to go back to her guests. Sadie and Margaret had decorated the outside of my place welcoming Mattie home, and were over shortly to see us. They marveled over Mattie, and at how beautiful he was. Sadie brought over dinner that night, and Margaret the next night so I wouldn't have to worry about fixing anything to eat. They brought enough food to last me a week!

Everything was going great with Mattie and me. He started to sleep through the night at about three weeks old. It was nice that I could get an almost a full night of sleep now. It wasn't long before I saw him turn himself over. Mattie's six weeks check-up went great, and I was feeling like my old self again. I was full of energy, and had made a schedule to help keep things on track for us. I had never been the type to make a schedule, but I had now, along with lists on things I needed at the store.

Summer was on us before I knew it, and Sadie and I

were back to sitting in the rocking chairs on the front porch together with our babies at night. When we couldn't enjoy the evening night we would lay a heavy blanket down on my living room floor to lay the babies there. They would look at each other, and jabber as if they were talking before they usually fell asleep. It was so nice having Sadie there to help with the long nights. Actually it helped both of us because Gary was on afternoon shift by then.

A base financial officer had come by with an insurance check for me that Matt had taken out before going overseas. I couldn't believe it had taken that long to be processed, but now I had it, and knew that the next day the bank would get it. It would go into my savings account for emergencies or such. I was going to try to live off what I got monthly for as long as I could, and the best that I could.

I decided I'd take little Mattie to go visit his grandparents a few states over. Matt had never told me not to, but I thought they would enjoy seeing their only grandchild they had from Matt. I didn't call to arrange a time, or even talk to them ahead of time. Matt hadn't wanted anything to do with them, but I was sure he would have wanted them to meet me, and to see our baby, their grandson. I thought I'd check the area out first before calling just in case it wasn't the greatest area, and boy was I glad I had. After I drove by the house I didn't think the neighborhood looked that good or safe to be in, so I gave them a call from our motel room. I thought it would be better to meet somewhere away from their house....safer.

His mother answered the phone sounding annoyed.

After I explained who I was she only wanted to know what I had wanted from them. When I explained who I was again, and that I had Matt's baby with me thinking they'd like to meet us. My goodness, I couldn't believe what she had the nerve to say to me. She didn't want to see no child of Matt's, let alone me. All she wanted to know was where their check was.

I was confused, and had to asked her what check was she referring to. She had wanted the insurance check on Matt's death from the military. I explained that it came to me, and our baby. She started screaming something that I couldn't make out before hanging up on me. I was stunned. All they wanted was the insurance money from Matt's death. Matt had said there was no love lost when it came to his family, and I can see that he was right. I was sadden at the fact that Matt's death didn't mean anything to them other than receiving a check. Or the fact they still had a part of their son still alive through Mattie.

I put my phone down scooping little Mattie into my arms whispering to him that we would have to be fine without them. Mattie cooed at me grabbing my finger as if to tell me we would be fine, too. I ordered room service for my supper at the motel we were staying at, and when that was brought to me I had asked the gal who had delivered it if she knew of the Milton family. She said she knew of them telling me they were the troublemakers in town. They had a son in the military that had been killed recently, and they didn't seem to even care about that. They were just bad people all around as far as she was concerned. I thanked her for her honestly, and gave her a nice tip before I went to eat my supper. I didn't think it was necessary for me to tell her what had happened earlier with Matt's mother and myself. It wasn't anything she needed to know. I fed Mattie before putting him in his portable crib I had brought, and he fell asleep within minutes.

I laid down myself trying to make sense of Matt's parents, what his mother had said, as well as the gal who had delivered my dinner. No wonder Matt wanted away from that place. It was the best thing he had done from the sounds of it. That would be the last time I ever go to that town, and I wouldn't worry about them being a part of Mattie's life either. I just thought they would have liked to have seen, and hold Matt's son out of respect, and maybe have some love for Mattie.

On my way back home the next morning I stopped in to see Helen telling her how my meeting with Matt's parents had gone. She was shocked to think parents could be that cruel to their kids. She had Mattie in her arms telling him not to worry that she would be his Nana-Helen, and kissed his little fingers. She looked up at me asking if that would be okay with me for him to call her that. I told her I wouldn't have it any other way. I knew in my heart Matt would have agreed with me as well.

I watched Mattie discover everything around him shortly, and when he got himself up on his hands and knees he started rocking back and forth. I knew it wouldn't be much longer before he'd be crawling all over the place, and reaching for things he didn't need to have. It was amazing me with every milestone he did, and knew he was achieving everything on time.

Mattie loved being outside, and many days Sadie and

I would take the boys to the backyard to let them play in the play area we had Gary make for them. We were able to sit and watch them play together until they were ready for their afternoon nap.

Autumn was starting to make itself known earlier than normal that year, and I needed to buy warmer clothes for Mattie, and for myself. He was growing out of everything that I had already bought for him. Sadie was in the same boat with Sammy so we took the babies with us to shop for them a few days later. The boys were so good, and people commented on how cute they were when they came over to see them. We bought enough outfits to last until Spring. Sadie said whatever Sammy would outgrow she'd pass them down to Mattie. She wasn't too keen on having anymore babies, and didn't want to keep things around.

The boys grew so fast, and played so well together. It made it nice for both Sadie and myself. We could actually enjoy our visits. I had a playpen large enough for two more kids if it ever came to that. Many times we'd bundled them up warm to take them outside to the play area for the fresh air. Those nights they both slept very well, and I actually got some "me time" to soak in the tub longer.

Christmas wasn't a special time for me growing up. I was disappointed more than anything on Christmas morning waking up to usually nothing under the tree for me. I wasn't looking forward to it this year without Matt either. But, I put up a tree for Mattie who had enjoyed the many lights our tree held, and even though my tree is decorated only half way down, he was still able to pull some ornaments off now and then when he got his walker close enough to reach for them. He didn't like sitting on Santa's lap not one bit for a picture, so we didn't get a nice photo to remember that day by. People probably won't think it was a nice photo of him with Santa, but I absolutely cherished it.

Everyday I see more and more of Matt's features in Mattie from the curly hair to the infectious smile with the dimple on his left side of his tiny mouth. I often wonder how Matt and I would be doing every now and then, especially when Mattie and I would visit his grave. I know Matt is still with us though. Every now and then I would take his last letter to read, and know he had meant every word that he had written. Matt insisted that I meet other people, and to go on with my life. I had a hard time with that sentence every time I read it. I couldn't think of going on with my life like he was suggesting. And besides, I had Mattie to think about, and his life was more precious than anything else.

Christmas Eve service at the church was amazingly beautiful. Mattie slept through the entire service as most babies had. The music must had been enough to lull them asleep. The pastor had the best sermon I could ever remember in a long time, but it may have been that because I was able to understand the meaning he was trying to convey on the spirit of Christmas. Regardless, it was beautiful. I left there knowing my heart was filled with the spirit and love of the season.

Christmas dinner was at Helen's house again, and as usual it was superb. She had several friends over along with a few guests staying there, so it was truly a Christmas to remember and enjoy. After dinner we sat in the living room talking about past Christmas'. Helen had said her husband would dress up as Santa to visit their kids the week before Christmas. He would put the fear in them that he knew if they had been good or bad throughout the entire year, and gave examples only a parent would know. It was always the best behaved time in their household after his visit, and we all chuckled. So many wonderful things people shared, and I knew I would keep some of their ideas for myself to use down the road with Mattie.

After we had finished eating our dessert we slowly but surely made our ways back to our own homes. Before I fell asleep the angel on the top of my tree flickered off and on several times. I smiled, and said Merry Christmas Matt, and it suddenly stopped flickering. I smiled knowing that Matt was my angel above before I fell into a deep needed sleep. It was a Merry Christmas after all.

# $\mathcal{B}$IG $\mathcal{I}$NVESTMENT

I t wasn't long before we were celebrating Mattie's fourth birthday, and my running around like crazy to just keep up with him all the time. He was so interested in everything going on, and investigated everything like only a little boy could. I had him playing T-ball during the summer, and we would practice out back getting him ready for the league to start up. He had just finished tyke soccer, and he enjoyed that as much as T-ball. I don't think any of the team players understood the concept of the game, but they kicked that ball all over the field! Most of the time it was so comical to watch them trying their best. Sammy was on all of Matt's team as well, and we would always be there to cheer the team on.

Mr. Lindy had stopped by when he was collecting rent one day asking if I had time to talk with him. He had something he wanted to discuss with me privately. I had invited him to sit, and poured a glass of iced tea for both of us. Mattie was next door playing with Sammy, so we were able to talk without any interruptions. He informed me that he was thinking very seriously about moving to Florida to be closer to his daughter and her family. Since his wife had passed away a few years ago he realized he needed the extra help now with the simplest of things that he needed done.

After several minutes he finally got to the point that he had wanted to talk to me about. He said that he had told Helen about his plans the other day of selling the triplex, and Helen had suggested that maybe he should talk to me before putting the triplex into the hands of an agency. Mr. Lindy had wanted to know if I would be interested in buying the triplex myself. He would offer it to me at a decent price without going through an agency, and without their fees added on. In other words, the fees he would have to pay an agency would be deducted from the price that he was offering, if I would want to purchase it. Mr. Lindy had said that Helen thought I might be interested in purchasing it because I had been talking about having to find a job outside the house in time if I couldn't find a means to make it by staying at home. There weren't many jobs available that allowed you to work from home in the area either.

Mr. Lindy was only offering it to me before making an agency choice because he knew Helen for one thing, he knew that we were great friends, that I loved living there, and about me being a widow. He also knew how I felt about staying in the community with my situation in regards of raising Mattie on my own. He would let me think about it for a week before asking me what my decision would be, and also during that time he asked if an appraiser could come through during the week when I wouldn't be busy. I agreed with that, and told him I would definitely think about purchasing it.

I asked if he mind if I spoke with Helen regarding everything. It was a big decision I would have to make, and I sure didn't want it to be the wrong one. He totally understood telling me how much he makes monthly from the rent, and it would be an income I would have without having to work outside the home, which I knew I would have to think about doing in a few months or so. I had put that off for years, but I knew I couldn't go on forever like I had been living from pay day to pay day.

We set up a time next week to meet again before he left. Wow! He had offered me to buy this place that was well taken care of, and all the things that came with it like the riding lawn mower, and tools inside the shed. I needed to think about such a big investment. Investment, that was what it would be!! I would have money coming in more than what I would earn working outside the home, and having to pay for a babysitter. It was a pretty good deal on the price, too. Actually a darn good deal on the price.

I got out my pad of paper from my table, and divided it down the middle with the Pro and Con sides like I do for everything else that was a big deal to me. I needed to list everything I could think of to put in the columns. If I was going to purchase this place I knew that I would have to have everything listed that I could think of on doing so. So far almost everything I thought of had been on the pro column side of the paper.

After I fed Mattie lunch when he was done playing with Sammy, I drove over to see Helen to mull over the proposition Mr. Lindy had offered me. She helped me with my list, and things were really starting to add up in the pro column so quickly. A few draw backs weren't even worth putting down on the paper, but the one draw back was that it really needed a fence along the back property line.

There was a very steep hill that went down to a river. I had always been worried about that since moving in, and especially after I had Mattie. Helen told me that she knew that her handyman could do that job for me at a very reasonable rate. Also, that Mr. Lindy had his gardener mow the lawn at his house as well as the triplex, and that he would probably be more than happy to continue mowing for me if I bought the place, if I wanted. That went on the pro side.

Helen had told me she thought of me when Mr. Lindy had told her that he was thinking about selling the triplex, and knowing that I was thinking about having to get a job in the near future. I wouldn't have to if I was owner of the property. It would have to take some dedication on my part to keep books straight on the place, but Helen felt it was a slam dunk for me with the way I was organized. And besides, I could use the money from Matt's insurance that was doing nothing in the bank but building a little interest that I could use to pay for it, and still have plenty left over for any emergencies.

Mr. Lindy said he'd provide me with his past five years of taxes and insurance costs on the place to help with my decision the following day. He was being very transparent with everything about the property knowing it would be a huge step for me. The best part would be the fact I wouldn't have to work outside the house, or having to put Mattie in a daycare center which I would lose half my salary for that expense in itself, plus the additional gas money I would go through driving everywhere. It definitely would be a great investment, and with the base so close I would never have any problems keeping renters.

The next day I went to the bank to see what would be the best option for me, if I decided to purchase it. The adviser at the bank agreed with me, but also said if I did finance it I could take the interest off my taxes as well as the unforeseen expenses that might pop up. Either way it would be a good choice if I went with the offer.

I sat on the idea a few more days before calling Mr. Lindy to accept his offer, and wanted to know when he would want to do it. The appraiser had already been through the places, and the price was in range of everything else selling in that area, and the condition of the triplex was sound. I had asked that all the major items like the furnaces, AC units, and appliances be serviced ahead of time which Mr. Lindy didn't have a problem doing.

By the end of the month Mr. Lindy and I had gone to the bank to get the funds, and go to the title company to get my name on the title. Being the landlady had several responsibilities, and with Mr. Lindy's helpful list I knew I would be able to adjust things easily to fit my style.

I went to Sadie and Margaret telling them the news which they were both very pleased for me. Margaret had news of her own which both Sadie and I were expecting at any moment. Her husband had gotten orders to another base, and they would be leaving in three months. I had already been told by Mr. Lindy that news, but mum had been the word between us. Mr. Lindy had informed me at that time when they move out that I would be able to increase the monthly rent on that unit by a good substantial amount, and the same when Sadie and Gary would leave. It would add to my monthly income with them moving.

Mr. Lindy and his friend at the bank helped me open a separate account from my personal use for just the rental units. I had to keep in mind that I wouldn't need to pay rent myself which added to the plus side on my paper when I was figuring things out. But I would need the checking account so I could make payments when necessary to places that I would probably need down the road for possible repairs. It all had made sense to me, and I was positive that no one wouldn't steer me wrong.

I had samples of the rental agreements that had been used in the past, but they desperately needed updated. I decided that I would need to designate an area for my office in the basement for tax purposes. I had bought a new desk, chair, file cabinet, area rug and supplies that I thought I would need. I set my office up in the basement close to the play area for Mattie. It was a perfect area for me to work, and to keep my eye on him at the same time.

When my new purchases had arrived the guys carried everything to the basement for me. I was pretty proud of myself when I had everything situated the way I had wanted. I was going to treat it as professional job as I possibly could.

It was hard saying good bye to Margaret and her

family when they pulled away a few months later, and I knew I would miss them. Margaret was a great friend, but military rules the placement of families. You go where they send you. They were pretty pleased about where they were going. Hawaii….. who wouldn't like that assignment!

I went into their unit later that day expecting to clean it, but it was absolutely spotless. I would be able to rent that unit immediately. I went to base housing on the base to put up a notice of the rental on their board, and before I got home I already had three people interested in seeing it. I asked them to come by, fill out an application after I had shown them the unit, and they would hear from me by the end of the week after I checked their references.

When they came over I showed them the unit which they were pleased with the size, and amount I was asking for except one. I had stipulated in bold letters no pets other than fish, hamsters, gerbils, bird, etc. I lost one applicant right away because they had two large German Shepard dogs. I had that on my card I placed in the housing office on base, but they thought maybe they could change my mind. Nope, I had to stick by my rule for the other renters, and for myself. To be frank, I didn't want to have a backyard with dog pooh all over if they didn't look after their dog. And my insurance would be higher with dogs in case a dog would happen to bite anyone, so I stuck by my rule. I had Mattie and Sammy to consider as well. I would be devastated if either one of the boys were ever bitten by a dog of any size.

One applicant consisted of three guys looking to share the unit. They were computer programmers serving in the Army, and had several references from former places they lived in the past. I read the references they had supplied that night, which seemed like they were very good tenants in their past. I would have to make a few calls to former landlords to double check them out. The previous landlords were very impressed with the guys assuring me that I shouldn't have any problems with them. They had never had any problems, and was sad when they had to leave.

My other applicant was a couple. I didn't get good vibes from the lady at all. She looked the place over with the look of holier-than-tho as if she was disgusted to be there period. She had a cheeky attitude the entire time she looked at everything. I wanted everyone to be able to get along with others in the triplex, especially with me, but I got nothing but negative vibes from her as soon as she was inside the unit. When she asked if I would be having the place cleaned anytime soon I knew then I didn't want them living there. Heaven knows what all she would complain about later, and drain my account dry in a matter of time over picky things.

After doing a credit and reference check on both applicants I had decided on the three guys as the renters. They had such great reports from everyone, and they even put their first shirt on base down as a reference. He had spoken highly on each of them assuring me that they wouldn't cause any trouble when I had called him. In fact, he said if there ever came a time that any one of them stepped out of line in any way what-so-ever that I was to call him, and he would handle the situation immediately from his end as well. But, he again assured me that they would be top notch renters. I thanked him for his reference as well as for his willingness to intervene if needed.

Greg, Andrew, and Charlie paid all the fees that I was asking for that night after I told them my expectations on a few things. One big thing was that they knew about Mattie, and that he was my highest priority along with the rental unit. I introduced them to Sadie and Gary as we walked back to the unit where I gave them their keys, and they took one more look through the unit jotting down a few things they would need to purchase right away.

The following weekend they had planned to be moved into their unit. I did notice that they didn't have much furniture when they were unloading their truck. It wasn't that I was spying on them or anything, but just looking after my property. I just happened to be sitting in my rocking chair when they had started moving everything into their unit.

They had bought new furniture, and it was to be delivered that day, but there was a mix up with the drivers, and it wouldn't be delivered until Monday now. They came to me asking if I would be home on Monday, and if I would be willing to let the furniture delivery people in with the new furniture when they arrived. They even offered to pay me for my inconvenience.

I had no problem with that, and told them they didn't need to pay me either. They said they'd make it up to me with a cookout the following weekend then. They didn't have to do that either, but I knew they wanted to show their friends their new digs as well. Besides, I saw they had a huge grill that I would love to have had myself sitting on the back patio area, so I figured they knew how to grill.

Their furniture had arrived like the guys had said it would, and by the weekend they were set on having that cookout they had talked about. A few of their friends had arrived before I went over with Mattie in tow. Sadie and Gary were already there with Sammy, along with a few other couples with small children. A nice group of friendly people. When one of the other guys saw me he looked around asking if I had brought my husband with me.

The backyard full of people had gone silent immediately with everyone looking towards me for an answer. I stood there like an idiot unable to speak. Sadie came to my side as Gary told them quietly that I was a widow. My husband had been killed overseas. It must have been a buzz kill with that information because after that there was little chatter happening.

I wanted to leave right then so the rest of the people could enjoy themselves, but Sadie and Gary said everything would be fine, and coaxed me into staying until we at least had our food. Gary had winked letting me know that was the reason he was there. Greg was grilling steaks and shrimp for the big people, and hot dogs for the little ones which smelled divine. They had enough other items to go with their grilled choices. The baked potatoes were warming on the top shelf, and they had enough tables and chairs set up on the patio so everyone had a place to sit to enjoy the meal.

Once everyone was seated and eating the chatter started back up like it had earlier. The guys raised a toast to me thanking me for renting this wonderful unit to them, and everyone cheered. Everyone had commented on the place being wonderful, and that it had plenty of space for the guys. Most of the talk was about how delicious the food was, and I had to admit that it definitely was. The guys went all out for this cookout, and I was glad I had stayed longer.

The guys were busy playing Corn Hole that someone brought with them. The women sat talking in a small circle while watching their kids playing. Sammy and Mattie were having a great time with the other kids that I hated to break him away. I had bought a large jungle gym for Mattie to share with Sammy when he was about three years old. They were having a great time on it. The women were very kind, and one had said that she was glad I had stayed after her husband's big mouth. I told her it was still hard for me at times, but no one except Gary and Sadie had known of my situation so it was all okay.

It was still hard at times, but I was moving on the best I could. It had just taken me by surprise that he had noticed that I was alone, and that I was still wearing my wedding rings. I told her not to worry about it.

I thanked the guys later for the invite saying I needed to get Mattie home, and quietly left. Mattie was so tired that he fell asleep right after his bath leaving me some time to unwind myself. I went out front to my rocking chair with a glass of iced tea, and turned some music on low. I wasn't there much more than maybe twenty minutes when Charlie walked over with two bowls of warm homemade blueberry cobbler with a large scoop of vanilla ice cream on top, and asked if he could join me.

He handed me one of the bowls, and as I was busy eating it he had apologized to me for that question earlier from their big mouth friend, Eddie. He didn't know that I was a widow either. I told him not to worry about it. I had just never been asked where my husband was before. It had taken me by surprise was all. Most people knew he had been killed before Mattie was born. He understood, and offered his assistance on anything I that may need done around the triplex that I couldn't do myself, and I felt the kindness with his offer.

I finished the delicious cobbler that was almost a tongue licking clean bowl kind, but didn't go that far. Maybe if I had been alone, I would have licked it clean with a chuckle to myself!!

Charlie told me a little about himself, and what they did on base. His parents were gone, and his older siblings were just that…older…much older. He was a product of an oops when his parents thought they were done having kids. There was over twelve years difference with his closest brother, and that twelve years was twelve too many. They had nothing in common what-so-ever. After his parents had died his oldest sister had taken him in during his high school years. She was old enough to be his mother because of the huge age gap, and she had a son herself that was Charlie's age so he had a closeness with James.

After graduation he had joined the Army immediately, and has had made it his life and his home since. He sees his family once a year at Christmas when he goes back to his hometown a few hours away, and a few phone calls now and then, but that was the extent of it. There really was too much of a gap in ages, so he basically was on his own.

A few other people were leaving the cookout so he

excused himself to thank them for coming hoping they had a good time before he came back to sit with me some more. It was nice talking with him while listening to the music, and enjoying the night. Once the mosquitoes started attacking me I called it a night, and went inside, and Charlie went home himself.

The next morning Sadie brought Sammy over to play with Mattie. She said she saw Charlie and me talking last night on the porch, and asked about that. I told her he just came over to apologize for the comment made about my husband, and he had brought me some delicious blueberry cobbler he had made. There was nothing more to add other than I had enjoyed talking with him. The topic of Charlie was dropped as we watched our favorite soap opera show together while the boys played with the cars and trucks in Mattie's room.

Both Sadie and I had enrolled the boys in a preschool at the church for the following school year to give them an extra start for kindergarten. They weren't behind in any developmentally stage of their lives, but we also knew that it would benefit them, and it would also give them more kids to socialize with. Both boys loved the two weeks of Vacation Bible School every June at our church, and had met other kids their age that we have had over for play dates, and it also opened our circle of knowing other young mothers as well for Sadie and me.

Things were going well for me, and my life was kept busy with Mattie in his activities. I enjoyed it, but I also was feeling a little down when I went to the games to watch Mattie play seeing other parents cheering their kid on where Mattie had to settle for just me. A few even had their grandparents there, and I could see how much love they gave their grandchildren. That was one thing Mattie would never have at the games to watch him. Helen came whenever she could to cheer loud and fierce for the team. Occasionally Gary couldn't attend the games, so Sadie and I sat together.

I was missing the male companionship, and the love that I had with Matt. There wasn't a day that went by that I didn't think of him, miss having his arms around me, and the kisses we shared every time we could. I had wondered how a man in Mattie's life would help him, or if it would make him resentful that his dad was gone leaving just the two of us to manage with the every day struggles. I think of the craziest things at times, and wonder who I was hurting the most. Probably myself!

I tried to talk to Mattie about it one day to see how he felt about me being a single mom, but he didn't seem interested in what I had to say. Gary is around a lot after work, and he plays catch with both boys in the back yard often. I noticed that the guys in the third unit would often pitch in by playing games as well. Sadie and I would sit in our chairs to cheer our boys on. With the shade tree in the yard, and all the trees along the property edge it was rather cool most nights once the sun started to go down after a sweltering day. We were all becoming one large family, and it was nice.

# Two Peas in a Pod

I spoke with Helen on that very same topic on how she had coped all these years with her husband being gone. She told me things were different for her as it was later in her life when her husband had died. They had many years together before he had been taken. Her kids were grown, and had been on their own for several years, but she understood what I was feeling, and why. Helen had kept herself busy at her house turning it into a bed and breakfast to occupy her thoughts and time. It had been a big change for her, but it was one thing that she had talked about doing before her husband had died, and knew it was the best for her to convert her home. She missed him many times… all the time, but she had no regrets in what she has done with her life so far.

She never thought she'd ever meet another man near

her age that sparked an interest for her, and came to the conclusion that she was perfectly fine with that decision. The many friends she has never forget to invite her to their functions. In fact, she felt she was busier now than when she had her kids and husband to care for.

I didn't know what I was expecting it to be like because there are no magical wands to twirl around to make things better when times weren't the happiest, and to make other things go away as well. Maybe I was just feeling the loneliness of male companionship. Maybe it was because Charlie was someone new in my life to get to know. I really didn't have any other person to talk to on this matter except Helen that would have understood.

I had told Helen on how I had enjoyed Charlie coming over that night talking with me on the front porch. But at the same time I had felt I had done something wrong by allowing it to happen, and yet I was feeling good about it as well. Such mixed emotions!! She told me I shouldn't feel bad about anything. I had been a great mother to Mattie all these years by myself, had been a faithful wife to Matt while he was away, and we had done great things together in our short amount of time. I needed to do something great for myself, too. It made me feel better whenever I talk with Helen. She had such a wealth of advice when I needed it the most.

My mother had passed away, and it was over a year before I learned of her death. She had died in her sleep, so the obituary had said on line. Her alcohol content level in her body was well over the normalcy. So in other words she basically drank herself to death. That didn't surprise me any at all. I knew it was either going to be her drinking too much, or death in some other means that would have been her fate. I probably wouldn't have asked her about anything on what I had been feeling lately even if even she was still living. She had a tendency to blab everything she ever heard to everyone. Our last phone call was not a nice one to say the least, and I hadn't heard from her after that. She told me not to call her ever again.

It had started out a pleasant conversation, but when she started on about me not wanting to date, or have a good time with her male friends changed the whole conversation sour immediately. I had told her they didn't interest me, nor did they impress me. She went overboard on the name calling again, and told me that I obviously thought I was too good for them.

I tried to explain that I wasn't interested in them being her choice of friends, and that I had a baby to care for. But she screamed a bunch of profanity at me before hanging up the phone on her end of the line. I bet she didn't even hear me say that I had a baby. I decided to give her time to cool off, or run out of money, and need to borrow some from me, but she never called back. I probably should have called her after a few days like I usually had done in the past, but I didn't this time. So I have had to accept the blame as much as she should on not being in contact any more.

I had never heard a word back from Aunt Mary after I had moved away, nor from her son Brad. I wondered if Brad had told his mom about me being in contact with his friend Matt. As far as I knew Brad wasn't aware that Matt and I had married, and that I was pregnant with his son when Matt had been killed. Neither one of them came to his funeral to pay their respects. They both had let it known that they were mad at me for moving away the way I had, according to my mother one time, and not staying there to help my mother even though my mother hadn't wanted my help. It was a vicious circle I had been dealing with. My mother hadn't wanted me from birth from what she had said one night when she was drunk calling at three in the morning to yell at me, and she didn't want to know anything about me. It was all about her and John. I couldn't understand half of what she was trying to tell me between all her slurred words. And truth be known, she probably didn't remember talking to me anyhow.

It wasn't until I had read her obituary in the year old obituary I came across one night on the computer that I found out all the information. A year later! I wasn't surprised, and I didn't even cry for some strange reason. It wasn't something I hadn't expected to read on the computer though, and I had to read it twice before I noticed she didn't have any survivors other than John listed. I was nothing to her because I couldn't be like her. It was sad to know she was gone, and she never knew anything about my life, or her grandchild, but that was the way she was. It was always about her.

Later that night I was sitting in my rocker on the porch after Mattie had fallen asleep. Sadie was having a hard time getting Sammy to sleep so I sat there by myself. That was when Charlie walked over asking if I mind him sitting with me for awhile. He brought two bowls of strawberry shortcake he had made earlier that evening that were piled high with whipped topping. I devoured it as if I hadn't eaten in months. As we talked between bites of the shortcake he told me more about his family, and how he was feeling so left out of everything lately. He didn't want me to think he was a mama's boy, or couldn't handle rejection when he was telling me everything, but he needed to talk to someone. It was obviously weighing heavy on his mind. I listened to him, and could tell he was hurting inside. I knew that feeling very well myself when it came to family.

I told him I was feeling the same emptiness myself as of late. We talked until two in the morning without realizing it was that late. Time had flown by so fast. It struck me that we were two peas in a pod when it came to our families. Maybe even three peas in a pod if I counted Matt's family in on the tally. I didn't have any one other than Mattie, where he did have a family, but they were leaving him out of many family functions as if he didn't exist. It was the same way with Matt's family as well. So sad families had to be that way, but it seems to be that way for many people lately.

I asked if he would like to know about what I had been through, and he nodded his head yes. I told him everything I could, and couldn't believe I had done that. It was so easy talking with him. I spilled my guts out to him, and thought for sure he would think I was crazy, but he didn't. He understood everything I told him completely, and was shocked that I had gone through so much as I had.

I see both Sadie and Gary's families often when they come for a visit, and wish I had been part of their family many times, and in many ways. You could see how well they all get along, and help each other when needed. All of the siblings have so much kindness toward each other it almost makes you want to be jealous without trying.

Maybe it was because they still had their parents, and that the parents were the glue that kept the family together. I don't know. But it was nice to watch them get along as well as they seem to.

Several weeks had gone by, and I hadn't seen Charlie at all. I wondered what had happened, or if I had scared him away. I was enjoying our talks on the porch late at night, and actually missed him when he didn't come over. Maybe it was the desserts he always brought with him! It wasn't like me to miss talking with someone like I had been when it came to Charlie. When I saw Greg come home one night I had asked him if everything was alright. He explained their squadron was on "twelves" which meant they were working twelve hour shifts the past few weeks. When they got home they were in bed right away totally exhausted. That explained everything. I told him to be safe, and to have a goodnight.

Sadie would come out when she saw me alone in the rocker after Sammy and Gary were asleep to keep me company. She said she was hoping that when she would peak out of her drapes in the living room that she'd find Charlie in her chair, but she hadn't seen that in several days now. Told her what Greg had told me earlier. She understood that, but I didn't. I had never had to experience it with Matt. When she told me the reason why they do that often, I understood it better. Maybe Charlie had assumed that I knew about the twelves from Matt, but I didn't.

Mattie and Sammy were getting ready to play their last T-ball game of the summer when Sadie and Gary finally arrived to the field with Sammy. They were always running late. Charlie showed up a few minutes later, and sat with us that Saturday afternoon. I looked at Sadie as she grinned, and winked at me. Gary quietly explained that Charlie wanted to see the boys play their last game, and to help cheer the team on to a victory with us. He wanted to see if all the help our little guys were getting with them practicing in the back yard just about every night had paid off. It sure had helped more than what they thought!

Afterwards we all went to the Sugar Bowl in town to celebrate the win, and last game where Mattie couldn't stop talking about his homer he had made, and how he couldn't wait for next summer to get here. Charlie listened to him and Sammy very intently not brushing off their enthusiasm one bit. He really took the time to get on their level. The team presented the owner with the plaque for first place, and he immediately hung it on the wall for everyone that came in could see it. He was at several of the games himself, but never could stay very long. Summers were his busiest time of year.

That night after Mattie had gone to sleep I went to my porch and rocking chair, where I found that Charlie was already there waiting for me to come out. The nights were starting to get a chill already, and I knew autumn was going to be on us in no time. As we talked about the weather, Mattie's game, his excitement and passion for it, and to the up coming holidays I thought how nice it was just talking with him. Simply plain and safe conversations.

Just as we were calling it quits for the night Charlie had touched my arm stroking it softly, and asked if I would like to go out to dinner with him on Saturday. I must have looked like a deer caught in the road with the headlights of a moving car, because he quickly added that the invitation also included Mattie as well. I told him I would have to think on that, but I could feel my heart beating a little faster already. I didn't know what I was going to say next so I just said goodnight, and went inside leaving Charlie standing by the rockers. Panic had started to creep over me, and I certainly didn't want to have a panic attack in front of Charlie.

I rushed to the phone calling Helen immediately telling her what had just happened. She asked how I felt about it. I couldn't tell her it thrilled me, but I also couldn't tell her it scared me to death which it had. I asked for her opinion, and she gave it to me.

She couldn't see any reason why I shouldn't go. Mattie was also invited making it less personal. Charlie was being kind, and we had a good friendship starting. It wasn't as if he was trying to pull anything over on me, or propose to me for that matter. I thanked her for the advice, and after I put the phone back down I wrote Charlie a little note leaving it on his door that night. I didn't want to face him, so I quickly went back to my unit to go to bed. When I went to bed I sure didn't fall asleep very easily. My mind was racing over the whole invite to dinner, and being with Charlie. I was almost thirty years old, but felt as if I was a teenager with all the thrills of a first date going through my mind.

The next morning when I opened my door to go to the store there was a note tucked in between the screen in the decorative ornament from Charlie saying he was glad I had accepted his invitation to dinner, and asked if this Saturday night would be acceptable for us. He knew a place that Mattie would absolutely love, and the food was really good. It was a place called "The Caboose".

Apparently it was a line of several train cars together on a train track that had been converted into a restaurant not too far from here. I wrote back immediately telling him that it sounded like a great place, and I was sure Mattie would love it, too. Tucking it into his door for him to find when he got home, and before anyone saw me, or so I thought as I went back to my unit.

It wasn't two minutes later when Sadie and Sammy were at my door with Sadie blurting out that she had seen me tucking a note on the guy's front door. I felt the heat in my face rise from embarrassment, and knew I couldn't tell her a fib.

It was never in me to lie to anyone about anything. I told her Charlie had asked Mattie and me out to dinner on Saturday night to go to a place called "The Caboose". The grin that came across her face gave me the giggles as I covered my mouth with my hands. She was happy for me, and wished us a great time.

I had asked if she had ever been there, heard of the place, what I should wear, if it was kid friendly, and so on and so on at rapid speed. She informed me that it was a very nice place, very casual, very kid friendly, and always full of people waiting in line to get in that hadn't made a reservation. Sadie thought I would like it, but knew Mattie would absolutely love it. That was Sammy's favorite place to go to when they went out to dinner.

That Saturday night was upon us before I knew it. As I dressed Mattie I explained to him that Charlie had a surprise for us, and we were going to eat at a restaurant together. We didn't do that very often, but explained it required his best behavior. As I finished getting dressed myself, a panic feeling came across me that involved Matt. I wasn't sure if I should go through with the date with Charlie. I didn't know why my thoughts of Matt just flooded in my head right then, but I didn't think it was right to be on a date for some reason. I sat on the edge of my bed crying, and cried hard. Mattie came in asking why I was crying. How could I explain to him what was rattling around in my brain when I didn't understand it myself.

I thought maybe if I read Matt's final letter he wrote to me that it would make sense for me, and hopefully help. I hadn't had any feelings for Matt like I had at the beginning when I lost him and for months afterwards, but they were resurfacing now. When I read his last line in his letter, he had said not to stop living, and to find happiness, and love again. I thought of what Helen had said to me. Charlie wasn't going to propose or anything like that. Just a nice dinner out with good company. I could hear Helen in my head telling me to go have a great time.

I wiped my tears, and quickly re-applied my make-up just in time for Charlie to be at the door to get us. My eyes were still red, and my nose like Rudolph's when Mattie had let Charlie in. One look at me, and Charlie knew something had happened that had spooked me. Mattie with his innocent little mouth told him I had been crying, and was so sad. Charlie came over to me asking if I wanted to take a rain check. I shook my head no, I had just had a moment was all, and I didn't want to let him or Mattie down by not going.

The moment we walked into "The Caboose" Mattie's eyes got huge. All he could say was "wow" over and over.

Charlie had made reservations, and we had been seated immediately. Mattie stood by the bench at the table looking the place over as if it was Christmas morning. Charlie hit a home run picking this place out for dinner with Mattie. I had to admit to myself that it was pretty cool, and that Charlie had thought about Mattie when asking us out to dinner.

The kid's menu was so cute with train related items which were the same things like a hot dog, hamburger, chicken nuggets and such, but Mattie looked it over intensely as if he was reading it. When it came to his turn to tell our waitress what he wanted he pointed to his choice. She smiled agreeing with him that it was the best dish on the menu. He was pretty proud of himself.

While we were eating, the train "conductor" came around the dining car giving away wooden train whistles to the kids. Mattie was thrilled by this when the conductor had finally stopped at our table. He asked if he could give our son the whistle before giving it to Mattie. I smiled stating it would be fine. Even though he didn't know Charlie and I were just friends, neither one of us corrected him. It wasn't important at that moment, and just watching Mattie face light up made it even less important.

Once we had finished dinner while waiting on dessert Charlie had asked if I would mind if he took Mattie into the other cars for a few minutes to show him the train sets they had assembled in them. Mattie was out of his seat faster than what I ever saw him move pleading with those big brown eyes of his. I chuckled replying sure. Charlie stood up and Mattie grabbed his hand almost pulling Charlie into the next car. Charlie didn't seem to mind, and I didn't think there was anything wrong with it.

When they had gotten back to our table our desserts had already arrived. Mattie could barely eat it with all the talk of the trains, and how he was going to be a train conductor when he grew up. I just smiled. Last week he wanted to be a soccer player, this week a train conductor. What next?

When we got back to the house Mattie was almost asleep. I got him in bed, with him gripping on to that whistle. I got some iced tea for Charlie and myself, and met him on the porch. I thanked Charlie again for a great dinner, and for a wonderful time. He had definitely scored big with Mattie. Charlie had said that Mattie was such a great kid, and I have been doing a great job raising him by myself. I needed to hear that because there were times I didn't think I had been, but if Charlie had seen it I felt it had to be true.

Charlie had asked if I had cried earlier because of the emotions I had about the date, and that I was worried about Matt, and what he would think of her dating. I told him I was still having a hard time to to get it through my head if I was doing things right by dating, or if I shouldn't be. He quickly said he that understood. I knew I wasn't going to marry anyone as fast as I had when marrying Matt. Things were very different now.

It had taken Charlie over two years after his break up with his fiancee before he could even go out with the guys for a simple beer after work. They had been planning their wedding for over a year when out of the blue she had decided to call it quits. He had been devastated beyond anything that he had ever been through, but he knew he couldn't just stop living. That took him a while to get through his head as well. He had a lot to offer someone else, and he was determined he'd find another love to be in his life. Life was too short to be lonely all the time. That made perfect sense to me.

We didn't stay out too long that night talking. As we were getting ready for me to go inside I wasn't sure if I should just give Charlie a hug, and thank him again, or what. That was when Charlie reached over to my face where he gently kissed me. It sent shivers down my spine, and when the kiss was over, I wanted another one. It had been a great night in more ways than one. I was feeling better about my life, and the need to live again myself.

# THE START OF A NEW BEGINNING

T he holidays were upon us already. Mattie decided that he wanted to be a pirate for Halloween, and he received a lot of goodies. He had such a great time going from door to door trick or treating. I had to watch him at the house because he had learned where I had hid his candy, and started to sneak some when I wasn't looking. Yep, he was growing up too fast for me!

We spent Thanksgiving day with Helen so she wouldn't be a lone, and now everyone was getting ready for Christmas. The decorations were up in town, music playing over the loud speakers every day until ten at night, and I started getting mine out as well to get with the season. Charlie was coming over to help decorate the tree after dinner when I mentioned it to Mattie, and he had asked if Charlie could come help decorate it, too.

Charlie and I started seeing each other more often, and not just on the front porch in the rocking chairs. The guys had several cook-outs all summer, and most of the fall with an invite to all of them with Sadie and Gary as well. We were just like a big family, and it was a great feeling being included with all of them.

One autumn weekend Charlie, Mattie and I had taken a drive through the countryside to see the color changes of the leaves, and to hike a trail. The trees were absolutely beautiful with their vivid colors on display in every direction we looked. We started hiking a few trails, and found one that took us higher up the mountain where we were surrounded by all the colorfulness. Mattie had picked a few leaves up from the ground so we could press them between two sheets of waxed paper for him to hang on the wall in the kitchen, and a few to take to school for Show and Tell. The air was crisp, and clean, and we were definitely warm with our sweatshirts on.

We enjoyed our hikes tremendously, and about as much as we were enjoying being with each other. I was getting to know Charlie very well during these hikes, and I was able to share more of myself with him as the time went by. It was a good feeling, too. I knew in my heart where this could lead to, and I was fine with that. It had taken me a while to get to this point, but I was accepting it now. It wasn't that I would ever forget the magic that Matt and I had together because I won't, but I knew I had to go on without him now. Matt would always have a spot in my heart no matter what. He was my first love, and my first husband. A part of him will always be with me.

I had feelings for Charlie like I had had with Matt. I

wasn't sure if it was wrong for me to have these, but I didn't think I wanted them or him to go away. Charlie had brought light into my life once again, and I wanted him to stay there forever.

I was falling in love with Charlie, and I knew he had the same feelings towards me without us telling each other so. We had talked about it one night, and I told him I had several concerns of where our friendship was heading. My main concern was about Mattie which Charlie had assured me he thought the world of Mattie, and that I never had to worry about that. Charlie felt by seeing me, and feeling the way he did for me was a package deal in his eyes. Charlie had said that he would never try to take the place of Matt, but he was willing to take it as close as he could.

My other concern was the fact that he was one of my renters, and it could complicate things if things didn't turn out good between us. He brushed that thought off telling me he would be better than most renters would be. He had absolutely no problems living two doors down from me, and he would always be there when and if I needed help with anything. He liked the fact he could see me more often, even if it was just a glimpse now and then.

His sister had called him out of the blue one night. It really surprised Charlie because it was always a one side phone calling deal with his siblings. Charlie was the one who always had to call any of his siblings if he wanted to stay in contact with them. It wasn't long before he knew why she had called though. She, and rest of the siblings were going to be gone for the week of Christmas this year, and asked if he had another place where he could go to spend Christmas. She hadn't say what they were planning to do, or if they were going out of town or anything. Nothing! What a slap in the face to Charlie! They could have asked if he wanted to come along, but she had made it very clear without explaining it right out that he wasn't included. He calmly, and with a fake cheerful attitude had said he had a place he could be for Christmas. I could tell it had hurt him, and it hurt him deeply.

When he hung up the phone he brushed his hands together as if they had been covered with dirt stating he'd be better off not going with them even if they had asked. He had felt uncomfortable around them for a few years, and it wasn't fun when he had to start staying at a motel for the week of his visits. He would only see them a few times during that week on their selected times as well. They always said they had other things they had to do, and would see him at such and such a time, and which day. Each visit Charlie had felt as if they were counting the minutes until he would leave so they could do the things they had planned without him being included. He said he was okay with it, but I knew he wasn't.

I quickly, and without thinking opened my mouth telling him he was welcome to spend the day with me and Mattie. Gary and Sadie were going to their parents for the week, and his roommates were going home to their respective families, so both of us really would be alone. Mattie and I would go to Christmas Eve church services late the night before, and then I would just spend time with Mattie opening his gifts with a special turkey dinner later. He said that it was kind of me but… I told him I wouldn't accept any excuse for not coming.

It was settled, he would have Christmas with us.

I felt it was rude of his family to do that to him knowing most service members enjoyed being with their families on the holidays. From what Charlie had said he made sure he always had a gift for everyone under the tree, and it had cost him more than what it should have, but he wanted them to have something from him. He wanted to be known as the good uncle and brother that they would always remember.

That night Mattie ate his supper in record time so he'd be ready to help with trimming the tree. He ran to watch for Charlie through the window waiting on him to come over once he was home from work. Mattie always had a good time when Charlie was around. Mattie asked me one night if Charlie could be his daddy like the other kids had. I told him it isn't that simple, but I couldn't explain it any other way than to tell him it was something big people had to talk about first. It must have satisfied him enough because he never brought it up again after that.

Our tree looked marvelous when it was decorated, and Mattie was so excited for Santa to load it up with gifts he would open on Christmas morning. I got the little elf out that night as well with little treats hidden on the top shelf of the pantry behind some larger items so we could do that elf on the shelf idea again. I had seen it in the magazines advertised two years ago, and thought what a cute idea. It really did work for Mattie to get his chores done without me having to nag him. The "Santa is watching you and knows when you are good and bad", had fallen apart the first year I tried that, so the elf on the shelf idea had worked, and I hoped I could use that for as long as possible.

I had most of the shopping done for Mattie, and wrapped while he was in preschool, and hidden in my closet under a blanket. Still needed to get something for the rest of my friends. Sammy was the easiest one to buy for. I took Mattie to the toy store, and let him decide what he wanted to give Sammy. I helped him wrap it, and put under the tree. The other gifts were going to be difficult to pick because I wanted their gifts to be special.

The next day I pulled out my cookbook on cookies so we could get them baked one day, and decorate the next day. Mattie asked if he could ask Charlie to help us decorate them. I told him sure. He ran down to his unit, and knocked on the door like he had done so many times before. Charlie let him in, and in a few more minutes he walked back with Charlie in tow.

I explained it was a tradition for us that we'd bake sugar cookies one day, and decorate the next so it was a two day commitment. If he didn't want to help that was okay as well. Some guys just aren't into that cookie baking/decorating thing with the family. But, Charlie was more than happy help.

It was rather fun that afternoon baking with Charlie there. He hugged me when we were finished, and asked what time tomorrow he would need to be here, and if I needed anything to decorate the cookies. I had everything needed, and thanked him for helping. We sat on the couch and watched "Rudolph The Red Nose Reindeer" with Mattie that night. I had to admit that I loved watching it with Mattie every year myself. It was a special time for us, and a great memory made each time.

The next morning bright and early Charlie was at my

door holding three covered cups in a holder and a box of goodies. He had two coffees, one hot chocolate for Mattie, and an assortment of delicious donuts to choose from. We sat at the kitchen table eating them while talking about how we were going to decorate the cookies. I had every sprinkle, dots, and confetti that you could want for decoration beside the different colors of icing. By eleven we were busy decorating while listening to my favorite Elvis Christmas CD.

Later in the afternoon when Mattie had fallen asleep Charlie and I had watched a Christmas movie together while snacking on a few of our cookies. It wasn't long before we were in each others arms sharing more than the cookies. His kisses were wonderful leaving me wanting more from this relationship. It was then that Charlie had told me how much he loved me, and how much he loved Mattie as well. I had then confessed my feelings for him. We held on to each other as if it would be our last time together. When Charlie left that night he kissed me one last time adding that he loved me again. I was in seventh heaven.

When I went to bed I wondered if I was making a mistake falling in love with another guy in the military. If he had to go overseas, and by chance not come back to me I didn't think I could handle that. I prayed that night for some sign that I would be fine this time around. Charlie only had a few years left until he retired from the military. I prayed hard, and somehow I would know if I was doing the right thing, or not.

Christmas Eve church service was absolutely beautiful. Charlie had started attending church with me several months back, and it was if he had been going there all his life. He liked the church, the pastor, and the community spirit he felt within. His faith had gotten stronger, and we felt as if we belonged there…together.

After Mattie finally had fallen asleep that night, I placed all of his gifts under the tree when we got back home. Mattie wanted to wait up for Santa, but his eyes were slowly closing around midnight. I carefully picked him up placing him in his bed before I bit into a cookie and drank some milk so Mattie would find it in the morning, thinking Santa had done it.

Charlie was amazed at how Mattie still believed in Santa. His siblings had told him there wasn't one when he was four years old, Mattie's age. After that he didn't enjoy the holiday as much because he felt it was all fake. I thought that was really sad, and down right mean of his brothers and sisters to ruin it for him. They stole the fun from Charlie's excitement for all the holidays after that. I hope Mattie believes for a few more years because it makes Christmas much more magical.

We were standing in front of the Christmas tree all lit up when Charlie told me again how much he loved me. With that he got down on his knee holding a small velvet box opened in his hand with an engagement ring sparkling with the tree lights blinking off and on as he asked me to marry him. He had promised he'd always love me for the rest of our lives. And that he loved Mattie as much, and would be honored to have him a part of his life. Charlie's eyes were full of tears when I had told him yes that I would marry him.

After placing the ring on my finger he scooped me into his arms, and I knew that the night wasn't going to be over for us yet. Not by a long shot. I wanted him more than ever, and I was determined I was going to get more. I pulled him into my bedroom shutting the door behind us. It was going to be the best Christmas for the three of us. I couldn't have been more happier than what I was feeling right then.

We fell asleep in each others arms after making love. Just before Mattie woke up I scooted out of bed to start our traditional Christmas breakfast of homemade cinnamon rolls and hot chocolate with tiny marshmallows floating on top. The aroma from the cinnamon rolls woke Charlie and Mattie about the same time, and they came out to the kitchen while I was finishing up with the icing drizzled over the rolls.

Mattie didn't seem to notice that Charlie came out of my bedroom, or he didn't seem to care. When we finished eating I told Mattie we had something to tell him, but he said he already knew that we were getting married. He had asked Santa to make it happen when he sat on his lap in the store a few weeks back. Charlie and I just looked at each other before we burst out laughing. Charlie had talked to Mattie the other day asking if he would mind us being a family together. Mattie had told him that he would like that very much, but went right back to what he had been doing without anymore talk. Charlie had tussled Mattie's hair, and Mattie laughed with us.

Mattie opened his gifts from Santa, and was very pleased with everything he had received. Charlie loved the watch I bought him putting it on immediately, and he bought me several gifts as well as for Mattie. Everything was beautiful, and my cologne fragrance was divine. I had never had so many gifts from anyone under the tree as I did that day, and all from Charlie.

Mattie had a few things that needed assembled, and thought he would do it himself. I thought that was funny because we all knew Mattie wouldn't be able to assemble anything by himself, but he felt he was a big boy now, and that he could. He finally admitted that he needed help, and asked Charlie if he would help him. Charlie was pleased with the offer to help. I gathered the necessary tools for them, and while they were putting the things together I stuffed the turkey, and had it in the oven before they were finished.

The football game was about to come on, and the three of us sat on the couch to watch. It was another tradition Mattie and I had always done. Charlie was glad because he loved football games as well. Not the same teams we liked, but I was pretty sure it didn't really matter. The aroma from the turkey cooking filtered throughout the house filling it with a wonderful aroma. I started the potatoes while the last quarter of the game was on, while Mattie and Charlie set the table getting everything ready for our feast.

Once the game was over we were ready to eat. I lit our special Christmas candles, Mattie said grace, and we started eating. I was so glad everything had turned out as delicious as it had, and that Charlie had a good appetite. I started to clean off the plates when Charlie said that I was to sit down. I had cooked the meal, and it was up to the men to clean up after the meal. What a nice treat for me! He said that was a new tradition now. Personally, I liked it.

I had baked a pumpkin pie the day before that we ate later. Mattie was so busy playing with his new toys that

Charlie and I had time to talk alone. He told me how wonderful this Christmas had been for him, and how he enjoyed every single second of it. He had asked if we were big on traditions, and I told him yes because it gave us something to looked forward to doing, and it was a few things passed down from other family members. He liked that, and would learn what they were now. He was so sincere having the biggest smile on his face. It also beat the TV dinner he would have had to heat up to eat if he had been alone. His roommates had asked Charlie if he wanted to go with them to their families for the week, but he assured him he had a place he'd be. We talked for hours about getting married, when, and where our wedding should be.

By that time Mattie was getting tired. He almost fell asleep playing on the floor with his new cars and trucks. The day filled with so much excitement had worn him out. I got him into bed after he said his prayers. At the end of his prayer he thanked everyone he could, saying he was glad that Charlie and I were getting married. I smiled, and Mattie squeezed my hand with his little hand telling me he was very happy. My child was more in tuned to life than what I ever thought he was. And to think he had asked Santa to make it happen amazed me as well. Mattie had said that this was the best Christmas ever before kissing me goodnight as I covered him up. Charlie was standing at the doorway, and Mattie told him goodnight, and that he loved him, too like his mommy did. Charlie was very touched by that, and came in to kiss him goodnight on his forehead telling him he loved him, and that he was happy as well.

It was the best Christmas since we moved here for

sure. Life was good and we had definitely been blessed many times over. Charlie and I called it a night ourselves and went to bed. The night was just beginning for us, and with every kiss I knew it would always be that way.

~

New Year's Eve came quickly, and as we watched the ball drop in Times Square in New York City on the TV, and we shouted "Happy New Year" letting off our poppers Charlie had brought over. Streamers and confetti were all over the living room. Mattie had noise makers, and some horns Charlie thought he'd like. We put our coats on, and went outside so Mattie could make his noise to bring in the New Year. It sure beat banging pan lids together like we had in the past. Many of the neighbors were ringing in the New Year as well waving at us and smiling. After we went back inside I poured Charlie and myself a glass of champagne, and some ginger ale for Mattie as we toasted the New Year, the beginning of wonderful things to come. I had a tray of left over cookies from Christmas we munched on before Mattie fell asleep. I was so surprised he was able to stay awake that long without me having to wake him to watch the ball drop, but he had stayed awake on his own. He was growing up!

Sadie and Gary would be home the next day, and we usually have dinner together then. Crazy as it was, we grilled steaks outside in the cold weather every year. Gary always did that honor so we wouldn't have to go outside ourselves. What started out as a thought had turned into another tradition for Mattie and me. Having dinner with Sadie, Gary, and Sammy had made it all the better. After dinner we would all watch another football game while the boys played with their toys in Sammy's bedroom. I couldn't wait to tell them my news on our engagement.

Yes, it was going to be a great new year for sure!

# I Do

I had to wait several hours for Sadie and Gary to
arrive home the next day, but it sure seemed like
several days to me. Funny how when you want to
tell someone something as important like I had, how
slow times seems to go. But, other days just fly by too
fast, and you wonder where the time went, and what the
heck did you get accomplished during that day. Well, it
was one of those slow passing days for me, and I do mean
slow!! The game would be coming on in four hours, so I
prepared the meal to occupy my time. I had the steaks
marinating since early that morning knowing they would
be tender and delicious when the guys grilled them later.

The snow was starting to fall again, and they were
those huge fluffy ones that fell gently from the sky. I
watched them fall from the kitchen window wondering
when it was going to stop. It had reminded me of my

apartment that I had, how the snow came down, and how grateful that I was inside not having to shovel it. I stayed inside where it was nice and toasty warm while watching the TV, and drinking a mug of hot chocolate on those days.

With only two hours until the football game would be on I saw Sadie and Gary finally pull in their driveway. I didn't want to rush over right away, so I waited until I knew they were at least inside, and some what settled before I was at their door. Sadie opened the door, and was surprised it was me by myself. I told her I couldn't wait any longer, and flashed my hand in front of her. She grabbed my hand, and her eyes got huge as she gazed over my engagement ring. She let out a shriek then hugged me without missing a beat. We were standing at the front door jumping up and down hugging each other when Gary ran in to the room to see what the commotion was all about. I just flashed him my hand. He immediately hugged and congratulated me.

About that time Charlie had heard the ruckus happening, and opened the door to join us. They asked when it happened, and if we had set a date yet. One question right after another, and even though Charlie and I had talked about when we might get married, we hadn't set a date in stone yet. Just in late Spring sometime.

We all went back to my place where Mattie hadn't even noticed I had rushed out for a few minutes. Sadie and I went to the kitchen so I could finish the last minute touches on everything before the game started, and it gave us time to talk by ourselves. It was then that I asked if she would stand up with me. Her eyes filled with tears of happiness. She said "yes, of course", and as we talked more the time flew by with the game about to start.

I was glad we had moved the dinner and game watching to my place. The guys could still grill close by, but with the snow coming down like it was I didn't want to drag everything over to their place.

I set out some snacks to get us through the game on the coffee table, and a small tray for the boys to pick from of fruit and cheeses. We were having a great time cheering our teams on, and we were pretty loud I must say. The boys had to cover their ears a few times. I hadn't been with two guys who could cheer on a team as Charlie and Gary before, but it sure was great to see them let loose, and enjoy themselves. They were some how able to watch their language in front of the boys, but I don't think the boys would have understood those words anyhow. I saw another side of Charlie I hadn't seen before, and all over a game of football on the TV. I sat back watching them as if they were two overgrown boys. They were really into the game.

After the guys had grilled our steaks later, and we were done with dinner we sat around talking about the game, how our Christmas' were, and everything else in between. Sadie and Gary had such a wonderful relationship with their parents. You could tell they were glad to be with both their parents. It was a good thing they didn't live too far from them, and could visit each other more often. Charlie told them how it came about him having Christmas with Mattie and me. They couldn't imagine how he had to have felt by his family not wanting him around. I told them we had a great Christmas anyhow, and mine was the best holding up my hand to let the diamond sparkle. They laughed agreeing with me to that.

That night Charlie stayed the night again, and while we were talking I asked if he really did have a good week without his sisters and brothers being a part of it. He said it had been the best Christmas ever since he was a little boy living at home with his parents. I was glad for that.

I know my first Christmas without any family was the hardest on me. My mother was to have come over for dinner to my apartment, but she never made it out of the bar in time. I had cooked a great meal with all the things I knew she'd like, and made extra things for her to take home. I couldn't believe there would be a bar open on Christmas Day of all days, but knowing my mother she knew where one would be open, and stayed there all day with her bar friends. After that I just planned on being alone, and until Mattie came into my life I was just that…. alone without family. Matt and I had never even had a Christmas together before he had been shipped out, but I had imagined if he had been with me we would have had a great time. Thankfully Helen had made sure I was invited to her place for dinner after my move here, and that helped my first year. I guess you don't really need your biological family to have a family with close friends.

Helen had made it home from her daughter's place a few days later, and I picked her up from the airport. As soon as she grabbed her luggage we got it in the car, and we were on our way to her house. I was eager to tell her my news, but she was excited to tell me all about her time away, and how great it was being with her daughter and family. I listened patiently as she told me everything she could think of. She finally finished, and asked how my

Christmas had been. I explained what happened with Charlie and his family, and that he spent Christmas with me and Mattie. She was glad I wasn't alone. As I told her everything I had tried everything I could to get her attention by moving my hand all over the place hoping she'd see my ring. And she finally did. She grabbed my hand looking at my ring. Bouncing in the car seat she let out a war hoop that had gotten the attention of the people in the car next to us at the red light, and they looked over at us. She waved at them with a big smile, and then her questions came like rapid fire one after another like Sadie had done.

She was very happy for us, and was thrilled that I had accepted. She liked Charlie very much, and felt he'd be good match for me and Mattie. She had said that right after I introduced them at the park one day when we were walking with Mattie. Her only concern was that he was in the military for another five years, and worried he'd be sent overseas like Matt had been. She was worried for his safety, and for me if something should go horribly wrong like it had with Matt.

I confessed that it had crossed my mind several times as well. I wasn't sure how I felt about that, but I wasn't going to stop me from being happy in the meantime. Matt had gone overseas, and didn't make it back to me alive. I honestly didn't think I could handle that situation again. It was so hard on me without Matt for the longest time. So far there hadn't been anything mentioned about overseas assignments elsewhere than here for Charlie. I just have to pray it stays that way.

I brought it up with Charlie one night while we were laying in bed, and he fully understood what I was fearing.

He was willing to get out of the service if it bothered me that bad, but I knew he shouldn't just because of me. It was his career, and he had already put over fifteen years in of his life serving our country, and with only five years left that I felt he needed to stay in. I also didn't want him to lose his benefits and retirement pay either. I prayed about it nightly deciding that I just couldn't keep dwelling on the "maybes" or "what ifs", and to live for the now.

With Spring right around the corner we thought it would be nice to start a new life married then. Charlie had asked Gary to be his best man. It was going to be perfect as far as I was concerned. And we were going to have a long happy life together as a family.

While the guys were at work Sadie and I were busy planning, and making the necessary appointments to make my wedding happen. Charlie and I had to attend a month of meetings with our pastor, but they weren't too bad, or as long as we had expected. We wanted to be married in his church by him, and it was one of the requirements he had himself to attend his classes.

Helen was right there with us several times with ideas knowing how my first wedding had gone. Her friend was excited to do the flowers again for me, and the baker for our cake was happy to accommodate our choices. Charlie and I went to her taste testing of the different cakes she had to offer. That proved to be more difficult than I had expected as they were all very delicious, but we settled on carrot cake with the top tier of lemon zest, since only Charlie and I would be eating that in a year, "as with tradition". Everything went so smoothly for us to say our vows within three weeks.

Mattie and Sammy would both be ring bearers, and Helen's granddaughter Susie, the flower girl. It was starting to be the wedding I had always dreamed of having. It was both exciting, yet nerve wrecking at the same time. I have been through all these feelings before, but it was as if it was all new to me once again. Maybe because it wasn't a quick elopement like it had been with Matt. I actually got to make plans this time.

Sadie and Helen went with me to find a gown that wasn't overboard, but wasn't skipping on detail either. I decided on a sleeveless gown with a tulle bottom and a heavily embroidered top. Sadie looked marvelous in the gown I chose for her as well. It was on the order of my gown, but it was in a pastel blue. Helen's dress color matched pretty close to Sadie's gown, but in pastel peach. I asked Helen to walk with me down the isle, and she was thrilled to be a part of my wedding once again.

The flowers I decided on were a mixture of seasonal flowers with plenty of ivy and streamers that would go with our dresses perfectly. The guys were going to wear their uniforms, so we didn't need any boutonnieres ordered for them, but miniature ones for the boys. The little basket for the flower girl held white rose petals with streamers around the handle. The alter flowers were the same as our bouquets. Sadie had bought several items to make pew flowers with in silk, and we had them all made in one weekend.

The morning of our wedding I was more nervous than ever. I had already been through this before so it didn't make sense why I had butterflies in my stomach this time. Sadie, Helen, and I had our hair done together at the local salon. The gals doing our hair were all next to each other so the three of us were able to talk the entire time there. I wasn't so sure about Charlie and Gary watching the boys while we were gone seeing they only had a few hours sleep from the bachelor party Gary had for Charlie the night before, but the boys would be playing together in the bedroom, and probably do fine. And they were.

It was time to head to the church to finish getting ready. Mattie went with the guys to get ready which left me alone for the first time in my place. This was the last time I would walk out of my house as Katie Milton. It was going to be an adjustment for all of us. Charlie spent most of his time with me since we had become engaged, so it wasn't as if it was going to be something totally awkward with him there.

I was all thumbs trying to get my gown on, but with Sadie and Helen's assistance I made it. I had shoes to match the top of my gown that I probably should have worn around the house to break in because I could feel the tightness right away while wearing them now.

Charlie knocked on my door handing Helen a gift for me. It was the most beautiful single pearl necklace that Sadie attached around my neck. It went perfect with my gown, and it hung down to the length I always liked my necklaces to be. He told Helen to tell me that he was getting ready to go upstairs, and would wait for me there. He couldn't wait to see his bride walk down the isle towards him.

I heard the music start playing, and knew it was almost time. Sadie grabbed her bouquet ready to go upstairs. Helen's granddaughter Susie was holding her basket of rose petals, and ready to go, too. She was pretty excited about being in the wedding. Helen had practiced with her at her house on what to do for several nights, and was sure Susie would be great doing her task. I presented Sadie, Helen, and Susie with a gift before they had to leave. A bracelet each with their initials engraved on top, and on the back with Charlie's and my name with today's date. They put them on immediately while thanking me, and then we were off.

Sadie looked so nice as she walked down the isle. I could see Gary's face, and you could see the love radiate between the two of them. Susie was next, and what a cutie she had been. She dropped the petals as if she had done it several times before. The ring bears walked a step behind Susie. Then it was me and Helen.

As we started down the center of the church I watched Charlie's face, and knew I would always be happy. Our love was strong for each other knowing we could conquer anything life had to throw our way. We had said our vows, exchanged rings so fast, and as we were getting ready to walk back to the doors as husband and wife when several military men came marching in making an arch with their swords for us to walk under towards the end of the pews. We hadn't expected that, but Gary had arranged it as a surprise for us. We walked under the arch, and the last one wouldn't lift his sword until Charlie and I had kissed once again. When we were past the arch that last guy swatted me with his sword on my behind. I was not expecting that at all, but it was the customary thing to do that as I later learned. After several pictures had been taken we headed to the reception area across the street in the park.

Our reception was held in the park where there was

a disc jockey waiting to introduce us as we all walked there. We had a fabulous time, and I don't think things could have gone any better.

Sadie and Gary kept Mattie while Charlie and I went to the beach for our honeymoon for a few days. As Charlie and I had finished our last dance together we thanked everyone for coming. As we were walking towards the car we were showered with bird seed from everyone. It truly was a wedding of my dreams.

Our honeymoon was wonderful. Our room was the bridal suite right on the beach, and I had to admit… Charlie didn't hold back on picking the accommodations there. We were able to open our doors right onto the beach itself. The beach was a perfect place to relax, and just enjoy ourselves alone. The water was clear, and getting warm already. We went to dinner every night at a different restaurant that had overlooked the ocean having fresh seafood to feast on.

# A Blast From the Past

T he summer had flown by fast with us going to all the activities Mattie had been participating in. Sammy and Mattie were best of friends, and Sadie and I made sure they were on the same teams for everything. We made it a special memory that after every game, win or lose, that we went to the Sugar Bowl for a treat. The Sugar Bowl sponsored the team, and the team players received an ice cream cone free after each game, if they were in their uniform. As dirty as they were, the boys were proud to be on display when we went in.

Sadie was expecting another baby, and having a harder time with her morning sickness than what she had with Sammy. I watched Sammy in the mornings so she could get the extra needed sleep. Gary brought him over on his way to the base. The boys always had a great time together. When it was time to "rest", because I had been informed that five year old boys don't take "naps", they'd fall asleep quickly after lunch. While the boys napped Sadie would come over to chat until the boys woke up.

Gary and Charlie set a family sized tent up in the backyard promising the boys they would sleep out there with them on Saturday nights. The boys were busy going in and out of the tent adding things that they had to have in it no matter what. I honestly didn't think they'd have enough room to sleep in it at the rate they were gathering things. But I would let Charlie and Gary handle that one themselves. One afternoon they asked if they could rest in it. Sadie and I had agreed that it would be fine, as long as the flaps were up so they didn't get overheated. We sat in our lawn chairs close by chatting while they slept, and we drank our iced tea.

Once Sadie started feeling better she attend more of the practices for the boys with us. She never missed their games regardless if she was sick or not. Some mornings she sure looked pretty green, and probably should have stayed home, but it wasn't like her to miss out being there for Sammy. I felt bad for her, and told her if she didn't feel up to being there that Charlie and I would take him, especially when Gary was working, but she said she didn't dare to miss watching him play. At about four months she started feeling much better, and able to get out of the house more often without having to bring her barf bag with her. She began to enjoy her pregnancy better.

The boys T-ball team had won their season once again, and we all celebrated at the Sugar Bowl together. They had brought the sponsor the winning plaque like before, and he proudly displayed it on the wall above their team picture for everyone to see.

The guys spent every Saturday night outside in the tent during the summer like they had promised as a mock camping trip with the boys. They had a small charcoal grill the guys would light so the boys would be able to roast hot dogs on a stick for their supper. And they made s'mores for dessert. We decided one weekend before school starts we should all actually go on a camping trip in the mountains by a lake. The boys eyes lit up when they heard this news, and couldn't wait until then. I wasn't sure how Sadie would manage sleeping on a blow up mattress, but she assured me she could, and would without complaining.

Sadie and I had taken the boys shopping for school clothes during the week. So hard to believe they would be going to kindergarten already. We were so glad the boys were going to have the same teacher. She seemed very nice to everyone when we went to "Meet the Teacher Night". The boys liked her a lot, and she showed them where they would sit, which they sat in their chairs immediately as if they were expected to do that.

Time was going by too fast as far as I was concerned. Being with Sadie lately I was getting the baby blues myself. Charlie and I talked about it one night, and he was glad to know I was ready to add to our family.

We hadn't talked about adding to our family before we got married that much. I wasn't sure at the time if I would even want another child to be brought into the family. I wondered if I had enough love inside me for another child. We did know that we didn't want a big gap between the kids ages if we had decided on it, as there was between Charlie and his siblings. But none the less, I knew I wanted another baby now.

Charlie hadn't heard a word from his siblings since last December when his sister had told them they had made other plans that he hadn't been included in. He left a few messages on their answering machine, but they never returned his call. He thought for sure they would call when he told them we were getting married asking if they'd like to come. We made sure we sent them an invitation as well, but no one came. No one even answered back. He called again after we were married to tell them we were married, and again no response. That was the last time he had called them. Sad to think he was forgotten that way. Charlie was determined our kids wouldn't do that to each other, or to us. He would see to that no matter what it took. There may be times when someone doesn't see eye to eye on something, but that doesn't mean they need to shut them out of the family completely. It just wasn't right.

Our boys were liking kindergarten very much, and their work was proudly displayed on the bulletin board in the family room in the basement with a few tacked on the refrigerator door. Sadie and I were enjoying the autumn weather sitting outside on the porch in the afternoons waiting for the boys to get off the bus, and in the evenings talking and drinking our iced teas when everyone was asleep.

Charlie had left for work one morning earlier than usual, and as soon as I got Mattie on the school bus, I felt sick to my stomach. I didn't think I could be pregnant that quick, but I went to the drug store to buy a home pregnancy test to see. That purchase didn't take long to get through the town on what I had purchased. Helen was at my door within minutes from me getting home myself. I told her I wasn't sure. I was going to wait until tomorrow morning to take the test.

When I told Charlie how I was feeling, and that I had bought a pregnancy test, he said he already knew with a grin on his face. My lands, that news went fast to him on the base as well. You would have thought the people in town had a direct line to Charlie telling him my every move. I wasn't sure I could be pregnant this soon, but you never know, and it did feel like the morning sickness like I had with Mattie.

Charlie and I got up earlier than normal because he wanted to know the results before he had to go to work on the base. After taking the test we sat on the couch together holding hands anxiously waiting a few minutes for the results. It finally showed, that I was pregnant clear as a bell. Charlie was pretty happy with himself kissing me over and over letting me know how happy he was.

Once he left for work and Mattie was off to school, Helen and Sadie came in for our morning coffee. Helen had picked up some bagels and cream cheese on her way over. Helen came through the door at record speed asking if I knew yet. Sadie looked puzzled as she looked back and forth between me and Helen until I said "yes" that I knew, and "yes"….. I was pregnant. They hugged me, and as we ate our bagels I called the clinic to get an appointment to see a doctor to get started with prenatal care as soon as possible. Sadie and I both were thinking almost the same thought that we hoped these next two would be close friends like the boys are. And we both hoped that I would have a girl as well. Helen was just so excited to have more unofficial grandbabies in her life.

Charlie called at noon to see how I was doing asking if he could bring a new guy home with him that night for dinner. The guy was new to the base and his wife hadn't arrived yet. I didn't have any problems with that. We were just having fried chicken, corn bread, mashed potatoes with gravy, and fresh green beans. I told Charlie I would get with Sadie and we could all eat outside while we could before the weather changed too much more. Charlie said that I should ask Greg and Andrew as well. Charlie told me he would just go pick up two buckets of chicken from Danny's Chicken Place on his way home. I told him I could pick it up myself so he didn't have to drive to the other side of town to get it.

Sadie watched Mattie as I ran to Danny's Chicken Place before the guys got home, and while I was gone she had baked a cake for dessert, and had the backyard set up for everyone to eat outside. It was going to be a nice evening.

Everything was going great until Charlie got home. My heart skipped a few beats when I saw who this new guy was. I froze not knowing what I should do or say. I was in shock, and felt like screaming at the top of my lungs for him to leave. He wasn't welcomed at our house. The new guy was my cousin Bradley, of all people. I think he was just as shocked as I was when he saw me. Charlie didn't know what to think about what was going on between me and Bradley. I swore I could see Brad seething under his breath as his eyes squinted tiny when he realized who I was. I must have gone completely pale because Charlie asked if I was alright when he came over putting his arm around my waist.

It was then that I told him that Bradley was my cousin. THAT rotten cousin that I had spoken to Charlie about so many times in the past. Brad walked towards me giving me a cold hug like he did when he absolutely had to greet someone he really didn't want to or like. The feeling was mutual as I stood frozen in my space. Charlie was so confused, and was actually not sure what to do himself. He knew how I felt about my family, and here he brought the one cousin I didn't care for the most in my life to our home for a meal.

I put on my cheerful yet fake hello the best I could possibly muster, and welcomed him to our house as I quickly announced dinner was ready out back. Sadie and Gary had the boys ready at their little picnic table, and the seven of us at the larger one. I had to get through this night no matter what it took, and hoped it would all go well. I sure didn't want to make a scene in front of the others. Sadie could sense something was wrong the moment I walked out of the back door. She seated herself next to me with our husbands across from us. That had put Bradley on the end with Greg and Andrew, on each side.

During the meal I could feel Bradley's eyes boring a hole into me. Charlie introduced everyone to Bradley adding that low and behold, Bradley was also my cousin that he didn't know about until they got there. Sadie shot her eyes to me putting her arm around me to rub my back. She knew how I felt about him as well as Charlie did. I couldn't blame or be mad at Charlie because he didn't know this new guy was the same guy off my family tree. How could he know? We had different last names, and dear Bradley didn't know Charlie's wife would turn out to be me either.

As everyone was eating I felt Charlie rub his foot on my leg. I looked up, and he mouthed to me that he was sorry. I smile back at him to let him know it was okay. I understood, and I wasn't mad at Charlie. How could I be?

The guys were cleaning up the table when Bradley came over to where Sadie and I were relaxing in the chairs by the make shift fire ring. He stood there a few seconds before he cleared his throat to get my attention. I was purposely trying to ignore him the best as I could. I had seen him approach us from his shadow on the ground. He quietly said he was sorry he had intruded into my life, but he didn't know who Charlie was married to. He actually seemed rather nice at that moment, but I couldn't trust him as far as I could spit. I just told him that I hoped he enjoyed the dinner. Under my breath I thought he better have enjoyed it because it was the last one he'd be having at our house.

Sadie spoke up asking him if he went home often. He told her not very often anymore. He found it was too difficult to visit there. Everyone had moved away or died, and he looked right at me when he said that. I asked how Aunt Mary was, and he said still the same, traveling more and more with her group of friends. He asked if I knew about my mother's passing which I had nodded that I knew, but didn't let on it was a year after she died that I had found out. Thanks to my so-called family for not telling me. His small talk was pleasant, but there was that nagging feeling that I had wanted to know more information from him.

Mattie came over to me, and when he called me

mommy Bradley looked like he had seen a ghost. I did the formal introduction of Mattie to Bradley. Bradley couldn't take his eyes off Mattie. When Mattie left to go play some more Bradley had turned his attention to me telling me that he sure resembled his friend Matt a great deal. I told him he ought to, he was Matt's son. Bradley's brain must have been turning somersaults trying to get everything straight in his head. He asked if I had heard from Matt. I turned to face him straight on letting him know that my husband Matt, had been killed overseas over five years ago. Bradley seemed shocked to hear that, and finally told me he was sorry to hear that news. Was he really sorry, or was it because Matt and I did what Bradley didn't want….us to see each other let alone to get married. I added that I thought when Matt was killed that the team would have been at his funeral, but no one from that group bothered to show up, or send any kind of acknowledgment. It was like Matt's life hadn't mattered to anyone in the military family that they had always talked about as being a band of brothers in combat and all. Ha… that wasn't that way for Matt, that was for sure. For the first time Bradley didn't have anything he could respond to with that remark. He finally stood up excusing himself to help Charlie and the other guys in the kitchen.

Sadie looked at me, and knew exactly that it wasn't good on how I was feeling that night. She let out a wow loud enough for only me to hear shaking her head. She was shocked that he actually stayed for dinner after seeing who Charlie was married to with all the insults he had thrown at me and Matt in the past. I was close to tears by then. I could only reply with a "I know" answer or a nod of my head. Charlie was so sweet by thinking he was doing something good for someone by bringing a new guy home, and it turned around having it not be so great at all. At least Charlie was understanding enough to keep the guys busy in the house, and definitely away from me.

For the first time I was counting down the time when this whole dinner would be over and Bradley could leave. I couldn't understand why he thought he needed to stay any longer. I couldn't believe that he couldn't tell he really wasn't welcomed here. He should have quietly left while they were cleaning in the kitchen.

Sadie jumped to that hint by asking everyone if they were ready for her cake that she had baked, and brought it over knowing the sooner she serves the cake, the sooner Bradley could leave, and he did. I don't think he could eat his piece of cake any faster without choking on it, but I knew he must have felt the tension as much as I had. I couldn't even be kind enough to see him leave when he did. I was furious it had been him from the very beginning, and I knew I wasn't going to be able to brush it off that it had been him very easily either. This was something that I knew that I wouldn't get over for awhile.

Charlie came back to where Sadie and I were, and saw me crying. He was at a loss for words, but knew I needed time by myself with Sadie. Sadie hugged me telling me everything would be fine, and it was a guest we didn't have to worry about having over ever again. Greg and Andrew didn't seem to notice anything going on which I was glad about. The guys played a few games of Corn Hole before calling it a night themselves. Greg and Andrew had a great time, and thanked us for including them.

Once everyone had left, Charlie had taken Mattie inside, and got him ready for bed. I sat out by the fire pit trying to sort things out in my head, but all I could do was cry. I never wanted anyone from my past to be in my present life ever again, and here came my worst cousin of all people. I did have to chuckle when I saw the look on his face when he realized it was me. That part was priceless, but even that hadn't made anything better for me.

Charlie came out after awhile repeatedly telling me how sorry he was for making such an egregious mistake as that one. I told him he had nothing to be sorry for. It wasn't his fault that the new guy was the same Bradley as in my cousin. I was just upset that Bradley didn't even feel a bit of remorse by not leaving right away, for not acknowledging Matt's death, and for not apologizing to me for everything he had put me and Matt through while we were married. Charlie totally understood how I felt, and promised that was the last time he'd have him to the house. They would have to work together, but that was were the line would be drawn.

Charlie hugged me, and we walked into the house together after making sure everything was picked up in the yard, and the fire was completely extinguished. I fell asleep that night in Charlie's arms. I was so thankful to have him in my life. Charlie was the most understanding man that could help me through any difficult situation that came up now. I never thought this nightmare would end, but it did.

A few weeks had passed, and I was over the whole

dinner fiasco with Bradley the best I could be, until someone knocked at my door. I wasn't expecting anyone. Sadie would always just knock once before walking in. When I looked through the peep hole to see who it was I caught my breath, and my heart started racing. I thought maybe I should pretend I wasn't home, but my TV was on, and I'm sure it could be heard through the door. I took a deep breath opening the door with nothing but pure hate oozing from every pore on my body.

# $\mathcal{B}$RADLEY'S $\mathcal{A}$POLOGY

I really didn't want to invite Bradley into my house, but he had pleaded with me to please let him come in so he could talk to me. He had some things he needed to talk to me about that he felt were very important. Important for who?? Him or me?? I hesitated for several minutes, and flatly asked him why he had nerve to come back to my house after the being there the last time. Couldn't he tell then that I was not happy that he was any where near me? That I didn't want him there? Bradley broke my train of thoughts, and asked again if we could talk adding that if I wouldn't listen to him he would understand, but he thought maybe I should know a few things. Important things. Was he asking for forgiveness from me? I didn't know, but I thought that was a little late if it was as far as I was concerned. That would be a change from his past attitude whenever it had involved me!

I slowly opened the door telling him if he had thought he could just waltz right in expecting me to be friendly that he was totally wrong. Dead wrong! Also that if he upset me in any way, shape, or form he would have to leave immediately because I was pregnant, and didn't need any drama disrupting anything in my life that had been happy before he came around. And it was just that, my life, not a life for him to boss me around like he had before, or give Charlie any problems at work like he had done to Matt. He had agreed to everything so I let him enter.

Being in the south, and doing the polite southern thing, I offered him a glass of iced tea which he actually accepted. I sat as far away as I could from him so I could get up quickly, if necessary, to escort him out. I noticed there was a look on his face that I couldn't figure out, and it was totally out of his old demeanor. That sneaky arrogant look he always had on his face in the past wasn't there any longer. He had several wrinkles that had formed all over his face, and the laugh lines around his eyes were just that, a bunch of lines. His hair had receded some, and a few strands of gray was poking through his dark hair, especially around his sideburns area. I noticed several scars on him that I had thought were from fighting overseas with his troops, or in a bar fight. There wasn't any cockiness in his tone, or in his actions this time either. Something was different, and I was about to find out what.

He started out by apologizing to me about the death of Matt. Wow!! Finally Matt had been recognized by Bradley. Again, a little too late in my book. He had no idea we had married until the other night when he was here for dinner. And he had no idea that Matt was going to be a father. It was still no excuse for him not to be at his funeral, and I let him know that the whole team of so-called "brothers" should be ashamed of themselves for that. They were suppose to be a team watching each others back, but with Matt getting killed I couldn't see how that hadn't happened. Maybe they were in a dysfunctional way I don't know, and didn't want to deal with that anymore.

Bradley actually agreed with everything that I had said by saying he'd never be able to forgive himself for not being there for Matt if he had known. He said that Matt had changed teams midway through the assignment, and was no longer under Bradley's command. Bradley sounded like he had changed. He wasn't the narcissist person as before. I half listened as he told me several things, but they didn't mean a thing to me, until he said his entire life had been a complete lie to him. That was what got my full attention. What did he mean by that? He had a great life growing up as far as I could tell.

His father that he loved so much growing up turned out not to be his father, but his uncle instead. Aunt Mary had gotten pregnant by Bradley's real father, his Uncle Brice, but Aunt Mary had passed her pregnancy on to the man she had married, and who had raised him thinking he was his own son. I was confused to all that father and uncle talk asking Brad to explain how he had found this out, and if he had looked into it more to be certain.

Apparently, when Brad was at the house one summer

when Aunt Mary was on one of her trips he had needed a paper for the military, and knew it was at Aunt Mary's in the safe. When he opened the safe at the house he had found several journals of his mother's where everything was laid out in front of him when he read them. He couldn't handle that information very well at what he had found out. He had immediately called his mother for an explanation, but all she could do was laugh over the phone telling him to get over it stating that he had a good life, and it didn't matter who his father was. His last name would have been the same last name regardless which guy had been his father. That made sense because they were brothers, but to pass Brad off as someone's child was wrong!

With all that new found information, and the chilling response from his mother Brad had quickly gotten in his car while he was in a rage, and went down the road driving recklessly, and as fast as his car would go. He was devastated, hurt, and angry with that news, and he was going to find his uncle to confront him right then. That was his Uncle Brice that was really his biological father. He was heading to his uncle's/father's place to see if he knew any of this information that Bradley had just discovered. Bradley didn't get to his house before he had lost control of his car going in the ditch at a curve in the road, and was airborne into a corn field. It had been a good thing that someone had been a witness to his accident because who knows how long it would have been before Brad had been found. And alive!

After a month or so in the hospital, several surgeries, and another two months in a rehab center, Brad had decided then that he needed to change his attitude, and his life around for the better. He realized his life had been a total sham, and wondered how many people in town knew this information that had been kept from him all those years. All he could envision was everyone knowing, and playing along with his mother. Talking bad behind his back not letting him know.

Bradley's so-called uncle/father came to visit him often in the hospital, but his mother had never gone to visit him the entire time he was there. He wasn't important enough for her to leave her trip a few days early to tend to her own son's needs. He really needed her support during all the surgeries, and everything else he had gone through emotionally and mentally. It had been no picnic with the pain and fear he had endured. He had been in critical condition for several days, but still nothing from his mother. Not even a phone call or a card that she was thinking of him, and wishing him the best. NOTHING!!

Brad felt he had been betrayed his entire life by her, and it was obvious that she didn't have a motherly bone in her body by not reaching out to him in his time of need. When he had asked his uncle/father if it was possible that he was his biological father, Brice held his head down in shame telling him it could have been very possible because they were romantically involved for several months leading up to her marrying his brother, and for about a year afterwards. During that time was when my aunt had gotten pregnant for Bradley. The so-called father that had raised him was out of town so often on business that his mother had sought attention from her brother-in-law, and they never thought anything about it being wrong. After a few beers they would manage to be in each other arms, and finally in bed. Bradley didn't know if he could handle that much information right then, so he asked Brice to leave. Bradley was overwhelmed with everything he had learned about his life that he didn't care if he ever woke up in the mornings.

I started thinking that this disgusting life style was running in the family deeper than what I had ever suspected. My mother and her sister were twisted with all their dirty little secrets. No wonder why they never wanted us around when they were talking when we were growing up. They had too many secrets they had to keep quiet about.

How deceitful Bradley's mother had been. She was no different, and no better than my own mother. They were all dysfunctional as far as I was concerned. I was immediately glad that I had moved when I did. Glad I never got involved with my mother's bar friends when she brought them around, and glad I was away from that town all together. I was sure many people knew all this information, but never spoke of any of it. At least not to me.

Bradley continued to tell me he became better health-wise slowly but surely. When he left the rehab center several months later, he had cleared out all of his personal belongings from his mother's house storing them in a unit locker on base. He took his mother's journals with him as well so he could read if there were anymore secrets which might have been written in them. Bradley didn't say if there were anything I needed to know right then, but did offer the journals to me to read for myself. I didn't think I needed to know anything more about anyone in the past. Maybe later down the road I might want to read them, but right now I wasn't interested.

Once Brad had gotten back to the base he had broke down mentally, and had been hospitalized again for several months in the psychiatric ward until he could get a grasp on his life. There was a pastor from the base, and a psych doctor coming in daily helping him to realize it wasn't his fault for his younger years or for the sins of his parents. They told him he had to make things right with all the people he had hurt in the past, accept the things he can't change, and accept the fact that there might be some people he had hurt so deeply that might not ever accept his apologies. He needed to be a bigger, and better man that they both knew he could be. I think they were the ones credited to Bradley getting better about himself, and accepting everything from his past as just that, his **past**.

He had lost some rank because of his bad attitude prior to his accident, the fights he provoked with his fellow soldiers, as well as the ones in the bars who he never even knew but felt that they had just looked at him wrong, and that he was trying to earn his rank back. He didn't have it where he wanted it to be, or to where it was before he lost it, but that was going to come in due time once he decided to clean up his life.

He had made big changes by accepting the fact he had been lied to all his life by his family, the ones he had relied on for everything. He had a life that he had taken advantage of, and everyone in it. It didn't matter to him who he had hurt along the way either. But once he made the changes he had started attending church on a regular basis on base, and met a girl that had accepted him with all his flaws that he thought very much of.

I sat there listening to him while I shook my head, and asked what he had heard about me after I left town. All he knew was that I snuck out in the middle of the night, and that I didn't want to be bothered with by any family member. He looked at me asking if that was true. I told him partly yes, but there were things that lead me to my moving as quickly as I had.

One had been my mother trying to get me to go out with her bar friends all the time, even after I was married which in her defense she didn't know I had married because I never had a chance to tell her. She would get mad, and hang the phone up on me. It was always about her, and then when I found out I was pregnant I knew I couldn't stay, and Matt and I had decided that I needed to leave.

Another reason was when my mother's boyfriend John had broken in to Aunt Mary's house while I was house sitting to get to me for what ever he had in his sick mind, that I didn't feel safe there any longer. If it hadn't been for the neighbors hearing the glass shatter when it did, and calling the cops like they had, I didn't know what could have happened to me if I had stayed. There were other things that had happened that had jeopardized my safety when it came to my mother's friends. It was the best decision I had made at the time, but no, I didn't sneak out in the middle of the night.

I made him understand that I've had a great life since leaving there. I did have an extremely hard time when Matt was killed without having any family support, but I also had to pull myself together, and think of our baby's welfare. It wasn't just about me anymore, and I had come to grips with everything which I had to do on my own. My friends, the base people, and church members were all there for me. They became my family. I had their support and love surrounding me through the whole time.

He asked if I would ever be able to forgive him for the horrible ways he had been towards me, and towards Matt as well. I told him it would take some time for me on that request, because he had hurt me and Matt so deeply. Bradley said he actually understood what I was saying by adding that he hoped I would in time. That was all that he was asking of me for now.

He stood up to leave thanking me for taking the time to hear him out. I did warn him that I would be telling Charlie everything about that visit, which he said that was fine with him. He was no longer the horrible person from the past, and he was trying to be as transparent as he possibly could now. I also didn't want Charlie to have any repercussions because of me at his job either like it had been with Matt. Bradley chuckled saying he wouldn't give him any grief. Besides, Charlie outranked him, and could do more harm to him if he tried.

I thanked him for coming by, and he thanked me for listening. There were more questions I had wanted to ask, but I had enough information now to gnaw on for the time being. And when he left he asked if he could hug me, but I held out my hand for him to shake. I wasn't that easily to forgive on a moments notice like that. I held grudges with people that had hurt me for a long time, and Bradley had definitely hurt me bad. Time will tell if I will ever forgive him, but I knew it took a lot for him to tell me everything he had learned about his demented past.

That night when Charlie and I were having our nightly talk before falling asleep I told him everything about Bradley coming over to talk to me earlier, and what all he had said. Charlie asked me how I felt about him being at the house and talking, because after that disastrous dinner that night he didn't think I would ever want him around me ever again. I told Charlie that I was hesitant on opening the door, but with the TV on, it was a gimmie that I was at home, and trying to avoid him. I told him it was a lot of information for me to hear, and I wasn't sure how I felt about any of it yet. But I was going to think things over, and go from there. That was all I could do at the moment.

Charlie said Bradley was a great worker for him, and eager to always lend a hand to all the guys. He didn't give any attitude to anyone, and he seemed like a very nice guy. But Charlie knew there was something deep inside Bradley that was eating him up after being at our house. Bradley had never shared what it was other than he that he had hurt certain people in his past so bad that he deserved to be casted away by them now. He never mentioned having any other family, other than his wife, before he had been invited to dinner that night. Charlie had seen him at the shopette on base with a nice looking lady just the other day. Wonder if that was the one he had told me about, but I may never know.

Charlie said to think things over, and whatever I decided on that he would support me and my decision completely. That was the way Charlie was to me, and whatever I do decide to do, I would let him know first on anything and everything that I felt.

The next morning when Sadie and Helen had been over for our weekly coffee, I told them what had happened with me and Bradley. They were both in disbelief that he even showed up, but they were glad I had heard him out. I told them I didn't know how I felt about it all yet, and they understood. Helen said maybe he did make the big change because she had heard that many people, men as well as women, who have gone through something horrific like he had by finding those journals, and especially after being in the car accident can change themselves as if it had been a wake up call from the man above. All we could do is give him the benefit of the doubt for now, and see how things go.

Sadie and I went to our doctor appointments together whenever we could. She was going to have an ultrasound done, and wanted me to go in with her for that. I really thought Gary should be the one, but he couldn't get away like he had planned. She went in after my check up, and it was confirmed, that they were having a little girl. She had thought it was a girl right from the beginning. Sadie was over the moon with that information. It was too soon for me to have an ultra sound done so after we went to lunch we went to the baby store, and she bought a few pink frilly things. It was so different looking at little girl items. They were all so gosh darn cute it made it difficult to decide on what to buy. I'm afraid this little girl will have everything she could ever want.

I had to smile to myself with that idea. They had one of the two larger units at the triplex with three bedrooms, but Sammy's play room will now be turned into a pink nursery. Sadie had a pale pink paint already picked out just in case. Needless to say, she was excited.

I knew right away when she told Gary that night because he let out a war hoop I could hear through the walls. Sadie had confirmed that was the noise I had heard, the next morning.

# Contest Winner

e had attended church on Sunday morning as usual, and once we were seated I glanced up and saw who was sitting two pews ahead of us... Bradley and his wife. I shouldn't have been shocked to see him there because he had said that he had changed, and was actually attending church weekly, but I never noticed him there before today. Charlie saw the look on my face, and saw where I was looking. He leaned in to me whispering that we could move if I wanted to, but I shook my head no. I could handle it, as long as he didn't turn around to see us there. I wasn't going to run from him. Not any more!

Brad may think he had changed, but I had changed, too. I had grown older and wiser the past few years, and would no longer let Brad, or anyone else ever intimidate me again the way he had. I had to after Matt had been killed. It had taken me awhile to get there, but I made it, and nothing was going to change me back to the timid person I had been years ago when I allowed people to walk all over me, and lived constantly in fear in the past. Not anymore!!

It was hard for me to concentrate on the sermon that the preacher was trying to get across to us that day because my mind kept drifting to all the things Bradley had told me the day he had come over to apologize. I felt I was being torn between the past, and the present when it came to him. I prayed right then for help with my dilemma in making the right choice.

Why did there have to be a choice to make when life was too short to begin with. We both had been dealt a crappy hand in our childhood. With my childhood I had known about it all my life, but it was later in life when Brad had found out the truth on his, or should say all the lies in his life. It was right then that it hit me that maybe he was suffering more than I ever thought of before. A calmness had rushed through my body right then, and I knew what my answer was. I looked to the cross hanging from the rafters behind the alter, and silently whispered a thank you because I knew then what I had to do.

As we were filing out of church I watched Bradley speaking with the pastor as he shook his hand. I knew what I wanted to do. When they were finished talking I raised my voice slightly calling out Bradley's name. He turned, and I could tell he was genuinely happy to see me by the expression on his face. He waited for us to finishing shaking hands with the pastor before they approached us. He quickly introduced his wife Carolyn to us, and I quickly told them that we usually go out for brunch after church asking if they'd like to join us. Carolyn was the first to say thank you saying that she thought that was a lovely idea, and accepted the invite for them. She never gave Bradley a chance to get a word in edge wise. Wow!! That was something new for Bradley! It use to be the other way around with him always calling the shots!

We told them where to meet us as Charlie and I had to get Mattie from his room yet. Charlie turned to me asking if I was okay as we went to retrieve Mattie. Told him we'd talk about it later, and got in the car to meet at them at the restaurant. Sadie and Gary didn't go to church that Sunday due to having bad morning sickness again. Sadie was happy to just get through church service before the sickness hit most Sundays. She was having a horrible time keeping things down. I felt bad for her because I wasn't too bad with my morning sickness. Sadie had it morning, noon, and night. It didn't give her a chance to enjoy this pregnancy at all.

Bradley and Carolyn were already seated at a table, and was waiting for us to arrive. When we walked to the table, Bradley actually stood up as Charlie held my seat out for me. He reached across the table taking my hand giving it a light squeeze. No words, no other look, no other anything. Just that light squeeze. I didn't jerk it away either, and I think it actually was the some what of a beginning of our broken lives being slightly healed at that moment.

Carolyn was a very pleasant person that Bradley had met in church before moving here. She had a good job on base in the finance department, never married before, and they had no kids, yet. She was quiet until she felt comfortable enough to add into the discussions, and then I knew where she stood on topics that had been brought up. Their opinions were much like our own which made everything flow easily. I thought she was a good match for Bradley, and I also think she understood the hurt he had been through, but not sure if she knew about all the hurt he had inflicted on others in the past. Mainly me.

Mattie's behavior was impeccable during the whole meal which Bradley had commented on. Charlie spoke up saying he was a terrific kid before I could say anything myself. You could tell how proud Charlie was of Mattie from the way he spoke of him which made me feel good.

Carolyn made a comment that she didn't see any resemblance between Charlie and Mattie. I told her I had been married before, and that Mattie was my first husband's son. My husband had been killed overseas while I was pregnant, and that Charlie loves him as his own. I stressed upon that bit of information to get my point across so that she didn't need to bring that topic up again. Especially in front of Mattie.

None of us needed to be reminded of that. I don't know why people think they have to make comments like that, but they seem to do it all the time. You don't need to be biological to be a good dad, and Charlie was an excellent dad to Mattie. Charlie was the only father Mattie has ever known, even though Mattie knew he had a father that had been killed while serving in the military.

After we had finished our brunch I thanked them for coming, but I wasn't ready to invite them to the house anytime soon. That would take a little longer, and a little more forgiving. As we drove home Charlie looked over at me taking my hand in his, and kissing my finger tips while smiling. I knew why he had done that right then, and I just smiled back at him. There were times when words didn't need to be spoken between us, but we knew the what and whys of the touches.

I don't know if I was drained from brunch, worn out from being four months pregnant, or just needed time to think, but I went in the bedroom just to lay down where I fell into a deep sleep. When I woke up Charlie had dinner started, and Mattie had the table set when I had walked into the kitchen. Mattie announced that Charlie and he had made dinner, and that meant I would have to do the dishes. He was pretty sassy when he said that, but I had to laugh at the thought that he had put it together himself. I told him I didn't mind doing the dishes as I gave him a big hug. I also knew Charlie would insist on the clean up anyhow.

Later that night Charlie asked if I was okay with the way the brunch had gone with Bradley and Carolyn. I wasn't sure if it was just an act on Bradley's behalf, and I felt like I was waiting for the other shoe to drop at any moment for some reason. I didn't want to let my guard down yet for fear of him hurting me again with his salty words like he had done in the past.

It would be a matter of time before I could totally accept that he had changed for the good completely. They say a leopard never changes their spots, and he still looked pretty spotty to me yet. Charlie said whatever Bradley had done in the past must have been terrible enough for me to not want to give him a second chance to redeem himself in my eyes right away. Charlie didn't pressure me into making any changes right then, but he also knew it was eating at me, and he didn't like that. He finished by saying that he was there for me any time, and that he had my back on everything one hundred fifty per cent.

Thanksgiving was quickly approaching, and as I made the dinner plans Sadie had told me that they were going to go visit their family because they had decided on not going for Christmas with the baby being due in late December. So Thanksgiving would be a better idea. I understood that completely. Greg and Andrew were going home as well for the four days so I knew we'd be alone once again. Helen had a house full of guests this year, and even though she'd be more than happy to have us at her place I couldn't put her through anymore than her guests. Sadie told me she would miss the dinner immensely, but I knew it would be the last chance to see their family for awhile because they wouldn't be able to go there until the baby was a few months old.

Later I thought about asking Bradley and Carolyn for dinner, but got that notion out of my head just as quick as it had popped in. I wasn't ready. I was still having my doubts on Bradley's sincerity. I couldn't shake that thought that nagged at the back of my head all the time. He had been wickedly cruel towards me for so long, and with Matt at every chance he could in the past.

I understood that it was the past, and that I should leave it there, but my heart refused to see it that way. I'm sure he was rotten to the core to Matt when they were stationed overseas together that Matt had never told me about. Matt was just protecting me from Bradley's hurtful comments, that I knew deep in my heart. Bradley was the main reason Matt had changed troops when he did.

All in all we had a great Thanksgiving with just the three of us, and it felt good to be able to watch the football game, eat whenever we wanted, and not have to dress up if we had company. In fact, the three of us had stayed in our pajamas the entire day. We had never done that before, and it felt rather nice. At least we were comfortable all day. No fussing to get everything done on schedule for everyone, it was just us.

Mattie started talking about what he'd like Santa to bring him for Christmas the very next day, as if that was the magical time to think about Christmas. Lordy be, the TV has had commercials about Christmas for a few weeks already. Mattie's list was huge, and I told him he might not get everything on it so he needed to pick out a few things he really really wanted, and leave the rest up to Santa to surprise him. He agreed to that by taking the list back to make adjustments. He wasn't mad, but he knew his list was stretching the limit.

At my next doctor appointment the doctor had done an ultrasound. Charlie was able to go with me this time. He face lit up when we were told we were having a little girl. We had tears in our eyes as Charlie bent over to kiss me he whispered "a little princess for him to spoil". I couldn't wait to tell Sadie. Now our little girls will grow up together like our boys had. Charlie and I walked out of the clinic, and went to lunch on base at the Officers Club. Then over to the Base Exchange afterwards because Charlie had to pick out a few pink outfits right away. I was worried he would want to add another boy to our family, but he was excited at having a little girl. I couldn't be any happier.

Christmas was right around the corner now. Everything looked festive and colorful everywhere you looked. Kindness was in everyone's heart once again which is why I love this holiday the most. We had made and decorated our cookies one weekend to get things started at our house. Mattie had given me his updated version of his wish list. He did a remarkable job at cutting some things out. I knew he had to put a lot of thought into it, but amazingly he had done a great job.

The local radio station was holding a contest for the best "Dear Santa" letter. Two winners, one boy and one girl, that would win a bicycle as their prize. All ages were encouraged to write a letter, and the winner would be announced after church on Christmas Eve.

Mattie had wanted to enter the contest to win the bike, so Charlie helped him compose his letter. It was really cute. Mattie went right to the point of his wish list, but added that he wanted something special for his mom and new daddy. I was so touched. We didn't get him a bike, but if he won one, that would be awesome, too.

Every afternoon they'd read several letters on the radio for an hour. Mattie sat there listening to be sure they got his letter. When they finally read his letter on air, he grinned from ear to ear with his hopes up high on winning the bike now. I wasn't sure what we were going to do if he didn't win though. There were so many letters, and even the ones from the adults that really surprised me. I had never thought about entering a contest of this sort, but I didn't think it'd hurt for Mattie to enter. I didn't get the chance to listen to all the letters that were read, but for that one hour a day, Mattie was quietly glued to the radio.

Christmas Eve service at church was in a few hours. Mattie was ready to go because he knew they'd be announcing the winner of the Santa letter right after church service in the park by the lighted tree. The church service was absolutely beautiful, and the people there were all enjoying the sermon.

It was towards the end of the pastors sermon that he had announced that he had heard of a letter sent to Santa that he wanted to dwell on for a few minutes because he felt it was the place and time. As he read the letter that apparently newspeople on TV had heard about it as well, I had listened carefully. The person who had wrote the letter talked about how he had been a horrible cruel person to friends and family in the past, and all he wanted for Christmas was forgiveness from the cousin he had hurt the most, and the deepest. That was all, no money, no gift, just asked for forgiveness.

The pastor said that the letter had touched him deeply, and that this person was just asking for forgiveness. I looked over to Bradley up front with the choir, and saw he had tears running down his face. I knew then that the letter was written by him, and it was me that he was asking forgiveness from. My heart sank.

The pastor continued on saying that forgiveness was very important to everyone's lives, and it would not only help the person who wrote the letter, but also for the cousin that had been hurt the most by him in the past. Forgiveness is what we need in our lives to make it whole for ourselves, and our family. Also for our heath because it wasn't good to harbor hate in our hearts. After a few other things our pastor had said, I had such a feeling come over me that I knew it was time to let go of the past, and think of the present and future.

I looked again to Bradley, and he was still having a highly emotional time standing there in front of everyone in the church. I was sure everyone had to have known it was him that had wrote that letter by then. I was torn at what I wanted to do, and what I should do. Not what I had wanted to hear on Christmas Eve by any means, and from our pastor in church either.

After the service we walked to the park immediately to wait for the news of the winners of the bicycles. I was heavy in thought as we walked there, and standing in the snow on that cold night when we could be home where it was nice and warm. Mattie was so excited holding his fingers crossed in the air. I saw Bradley and Carolyn standing not too far away from us. I walked over to them, and put my arms around Bradley's waist giving him a squeeze. He turned towards me with his eyes still wet from earlier, and smiled.

That was when I reached up bringing him to me to give him a hug. He hugged me back, and lost it right there in front of everyone thanking me for the forgiveness that he needed. He whispered that his Christmas wish had now been answered, and he was happy. Told me how sorry he was again even though the road to getting there was bumpy, he was glad we found it in our hearts to make it a little smoother between us.

I think everyone knew by then that he had wrote that letter, and I was the cousin that he had spoken of in it. There was a hush in the air as the radio disc jockey took to the mic to announce the winners. All the kids were squealing with excitement. The girl's letter had been read first. She jumped up and down half running towards the front to receive her bike. She was so happy.

Mattie turned to look at me, and I could see he knew then that he might not have won. There wasn't any anger in his face when they had announced that Bradley's letter had won for the male selection. Everyone was looking our way, and cheered for Brad. Mattie had seen what I had done as I put my arm around him, and he cheered for him also like I had hoped he would. Mattie understood some things are more important than a bike.

Bradley walked up to claim the boy's bicycle, but when he went past Mattie he grabbed his hand, and led him up front with him. Bradley thanked everyone. He continued with his short speech saying his letter to Santa was heard by the right people tonight, and his wish had came true. With that he told Mattie that he had his choice of the boy's bike to pick from because he was giving it to him.

Mattie got the hugest smile on his face as he chose the red one, because he knew his father's favorite color was red. I had my hands covering my mouth with tears in my eyes. When Bradley looked our way I mouthed a thank-you to him. Charlie put his arms around me kissing the top of my head just as the church bells had started ringing. It was midnight, and it was officially Christmas. At that same time my wish came true, not only did I have a great family with Mattie and Charlie, now with Bradley a part of it, but it also started to snow again. Bradley came over to Charlie and me, and I knew then that I wanted both him and Carolyn over for dinner the next day.

Mattie had gotten us up at the butt crack of dawn to see if Santa had come. When he peeked around the corner of the living room, and saw that he had indeed come, he bolted to our room to wake us up. We could hear his feet hitting the floor with every step he took. Everything was going great with us having the most wonderful Christmas ever. Christmas dinner was a success, and everyone had liked all their gifts. Charlie took the bike to the basement to put training wheels on so Mattie could ride it down there until Spring. While Mattie played with his new toys the rest of us sat around talking about everything under the moon. It felt good like it should be with family.

Once Brad and Carolyn had left, Charlie and I put everything else away, and headed to bed ourselves. It had been a long two days, and baby girl was kicking up a storm for me to lay down. Charlie rubbed my back and belly as we talked, and how that within the past few weeks of our lives we had gone to having just a small circle of close friends that we considered family, but actually adding real family to our circle. We talked longer than what we thought we would, but it felt good to talk about Bradley without hate spewing out of my mouth any longer.

I think everything that happened between Bradley and me had been said, and it actually felt good to have it off my chest after all these years. I didn't have to worry if I ran into him at the store on what I would do, if he came to the house again without me being angry, and everything else in general. It didn't take me much longer after that talk that I fell asleep. A nice deep calm sleep which I so needed.

While the guys were working on base Sadie came over with Sammy to play with Mattie once the holidays were over. We have been so fortunate to have such close friends, and we enjoyed hearing the boys talking and laughing together. I walked in quietly on the boys one afternoon when Mattie was telling Sammy about his birth dad. Bradley had told him he had known his daddy when he was in the military, and told him all sorts of great things Matt had done, but the biggest impact on Mattie was when Bradley told him that his daddy was a true hero. Mattie was telling Sammy about what his dad had done to earn that title, and how important it was for him to always remember that.

I leaned against the door jam putting on hand on my heart. I had told Mattie about his dad, but when it came from another person that actually knew him in the Army meant so much more to him. I wish we had more photos of Matt, but we didn't. Mattie had asked Bradley if he had any that he could see. Bradley said he did have a few, and when he found them he would be sure to give them to him. Mattie had a new friend in Bradley, and I was sure Bradley would continue talking to Mattie about his daddy in a positive way.

We went to Gary and Sadie's place to bring in the New Year. Just as we sat down to watch the ball drop, and to enjoy the music, Sadie had looked over to Gary with her eyes huge. Not only did she look at Gary, but when she had stood up, her water had broke. We all laughed as we helped her get things together for Gary to take her to the hospital. Sammy would stay with us, and they were off.

Charlie and I put things away while Sammy got his pajamas, and tomorrows clothes he would need before we headed back to our house to finish watching the New

Year come in. I couldn't help but laugh again at Sadie's expression when her water had broke. We told them they needed to call with the good news as soon as possible. It was about four in the morning when they called telling us their little baby girl had been born. She was the first baby born in the New Year. They'd call back about nine to tell Sammy. Mother and baby Marie were fine, and that was all we needed to know right then. I knew my time would be coming in about two and a half months. Then Sadie and I could sit with both babies like we did when we had done with the boys.

# Moving Back

T he years had flown by faster than what I had liked them to. Charlie and I were still living in the triplex, but only for a few more years. The rooms seemed to be getting smaller and smaller on us with all the baby things, and Mattie's toys. The basement was where we had allowed the toys to be to kept since Mattie had lost his play room to his sister.

We had drove to Charlie's hometown after Charlotte Ann was a few months old hoping to rekindle with his siblings, but right away we could feel the scrutiny as their visit with us with the distinct vibes we had felt. They didn't want anything to do with Charlie, let alone with his family, without saying it in so many words. We knew what they weren't able to say openly.

We ended up spending the night in a nice motel on the outskirts of the town hoping they would come by at some time, but they hadn't, and we were gone without giving them a second thought late the next morning. At least Mattie was able to have some fun in the pool at the motel while we were there where he had questioned me about the other people he had just met.

Mattie was the one who had felt the cold reception we had received when we had arrived. He was very wise to his surroundings. He had asked me who they were when we were in the pool by ourselves. I told them they were Charlie's siblings. His brow crinkled up, and I could see it in his eyes that he was pondering why they had been distant towards us, especially towards their own brother.

Mattie had overheard two of the adults talking in the kitchen remarking that Charlie couldn't possibly be his father because there was absolutely no family resemblance, and had been stating that I must have had another man's baby while he was deployed. Mattie had quickly ducked behind the door so he wouldn't be seen, and made his way outside with the other younger kids without being noticed. Mattie had known enough not to say anything to them or to Charlie at that time, but he had wanted me to know that he knew Charlie wasn't his biological father, but he was his still his dad, and he always would be.

I gave him a big hug right then. Mattie understood things more than most boys his age had absolutely no clue about. I asked Mattie not to mention it to Charlie until the time was right, and it wasn't the right time at that moment. Charlie was upset enough with his family's cold reception towards us, and I knew this would tilt him over the edge on his emotions.

Charlie was antsy to get away from there the next morning. It was easy to tell Charlie had been upset and hurt by his family. We ate the continental breakfast in our room that the motel had offered before we pulled out to go back home. I could tell Charlie had hoped someone in his family would have come by yet, but when no one had shown up, he just shook his head with sadness written all over his face. He knew where he stood with them now. Charlie had done nothing wrong what-so-ever, but they apparently didn't see it that way.

I was hoping they would want to get together with us when Charlie retires from the Army in a few months, but I just knew that wouldn't be happening, and pushed that notion to the back of my mind until the time got closer. He was the only sibling they had that had served for his country, and the first one in the family to retire from a career field he loved at such a young age.

I decided I would send them an invitation to the ceremony, and let the ball be in their court on them attending the ceremony or not. I was determined I would make it a great retirement ceremony for Charlie, with or without his siblings present.

Sadie and Gary had moved back to their hometown earlier in the year after Gary had retired from the military, but we knew we'd always remain in contact with them, and we have. We had such a deep friendship with them that I don't think it could ever be changed. They were more like family to us, and we treasured them dearly. A family neither Charlie nor I had ourselves.

It was the saddest day of our lives when they pulled away from the triplex. I didn't want them to leave, but I knew they had family waiting for them, and they had decided that they had been away from family too long already. I understood, but it didn't make it any easier for me. I had a hard time with Sadie leaving. She was my first best friend close to my age that I ever had. Helen was the motherly figure in our lives, and we were close, but not like it was with Sadie and myself. I don't think there was a day that had gone by that Sadie and I hadn't talk on the phone. The phone calls weren't the same as we had at the triplex on the front porch in person, but they were nice. We missed them being right next door all the time.

Our kids were connected by that strong bond they had as well. We'd get together a couple times during the year with them either at our place or theirs. Several times we had met them at places we knew the kids would enjoy.

Several times we had met at the beach on long holiday weekends to get together. We shared an Airbnb that was right on the beach just last month. It was as if we had never left the triplex when we were together.

During the fall Gary and Charlie had taken the boys camping for a weekend. Charlie had said that in a few years the boys would be old enough to take on a hunting trip which he couldn't wait to go on himself. Mattie was pretty excited about that. I wasn't sure how I felt about it, but I knew Charlie loved to hunt, and whatever Charlie wanted to do, he had always included Mattie in with the plans as well.

It wasn't that long before Gary and Sadie had called to tell us that they were moving back to our town. The job situation wasn't what they had hoped it would be in their town, and they were going through their savings every month just to get by. They had given it almost a full year in their hometown before they had decided on what they really needed and wanted to do.

You could just imagine how happy that made me. It was selfish on my part, but I missed Sadie and Gary that much. Our families were so close over the years. It wasn't the same without them here.

Gary had applied for a position as a civil service employee on base through the internet. Charlie was glad to hear that, and when Gary told him that he was glad because they would be working together again. That made it even better yet. They were going to come for a weekend to house hunt, and I offered for them to stay with us with 'no' not being an option. Sadie and I were so excited about them moving back. We talked for hours about it.

After Charlie had finally retired from the Army, we had bought a larger house keeping the triplex we had to rent to other military families. That was one investment that I had done with Matt's money that I'd never regret doing, and glad I had done it. It had helped me in more ways than one. If I hadn't bought it I would have never met Charlie either.

Just before Sadie and Gary came to house hunt, the neighbor lady Rose had told me that they were getting things ready to put their house on the market because her husband received orders to another base. I jumped at the chance to tell her that we had friends that were coming that very weekend to house hunt. She asked if I thought they might be interested in looking at their house. It was a good size home, well kept, and the best part was that it was right next door to us! Was she crazy to think otherwise??

I called Sadie immediately to tell her about the house, and she was excited to look at it. I had taken pictures of the inside which I had sent to Sadie as soon as I got back home. They loved everything about the house from the pictures, but wanted to see it for themselves. I gave Sadie the phone number so she could call to set up a time with Rose and her husband for that Saturday morning. Rose and her husband had agreed not to put it in the hands of a real estate company until after Sadie and Gary had a chance to look at it.

I couldn't wait for Sadie and Gary to arrive, and I was on pins and needles while they were looking through the neighbor's house. They sure were taking their sweet ole time looking at it, but when they finally returned back to our house they told us they had decided that they would purchase it. Gary chuckled that it was the fastest house hunting he has ever done in his entire life. They thought it was perfect, and it checked all their boxes of wants and needs on their list. I was so happy for them. I was ecstatic that Sadie and I would be back together once again with our families.

I watched as the movers packed Rose's house up for their move a month later. I knew Sadie and Gary were anxious to move in. It was three days until Sadie and Gary would get the keys. Sadie had said the minute they heard that Gary got the job he had applied for on base, she began packing boxes daily. She couldn't wait to move back. I couldn't wait either. None of us could wait!

Once Gary and Sadie had the house and keys in their hands we all pitched in to move everything inside. Both trucks they had rented were unloaded with the unpacking of the boxes waiting until the next day. By the time the guys got back from having to return the trucks, it was too late to start unpacking anyhow. Everyone was pretty tired, and definitely hungry. It had been a long day!

Later that night I was sitting on my front porch with a glass of iced tea when Sadie had come out. Everyone else were sound asleep from the hard day they had put in from the unloading of the trucks. I had a feeling she'd be coming out, and had another glass of iced tea waiting for her. I could tell she was tired, but not tired enough to fall asleep. She somehow knew I would still up, or at least she was hoping I was. When we started talking it was as if we had never been apart for the past year.

Early the next morning after breakfast I had helped Sadie open boxes, and put things away while the guys worked in the shed, and in the garage with Gary's stuff. And I kid you not when I say 'stuff' because Gary had so many things that I had no clue to what they were even used for. After a few trips to the hardware store they had everything organized, and put in place. They could now put their vehicles in the garage with room to spare.

When the guys went to work on Monday, I had helped Sadie finish with the unpacking. I did the unpacking and smashing down the boxes while she put other things away. The guys were able to put the beds together the day before, but they weren't made yet. No one could find the box with the sheets inside. I finally found the unmarked box with all the linens packed in, and went to work making all the beds, and put the rest in the linen closet for Sadie.

That weekend we had a huge cookout welcoming

them back. Helen was happy to see them as well as everyone else who came. Helen was glad for me. She knew how miserable I had been when Sadie had moved away. Sammy and Marie called Helen, Nana-Helen, like my kids do, and Helen loved it.

It was a few weeks later when everyone else was asleep that Sadie and I sat on the porch talking when she told me how happy they were once again. Their lives were finally in balance, and they weren't spinning out of control any longer.

Their move back home after Gary had retired was really great at first, but then they started noticing that they weren't on the same page as everyone else there. I asked her to explain what she meant by that.

She said it wasn't like what they had thought it would be like. It was as if everyone felt obligated to invite them over when the family got together. It wasn't as smooth as it should have been being that they were all family. It was great one on one with their parents, but it was as if the siblings weren't really fond of them being there for some reason. Kinda like two's company, and three's a crowd feeling. And their parents had to divide their time with another sibling now which the siblings didn't seem to like.

Gary had been the first to mention it out loud even though Sadie had felt it herself beforehand. She didn't want to bring it up to Gary because he seemed happy, or so she had thought he was.

Apparently his brother had made several wisecracks about Gary getting extra money from the government for his retirement, how Gary didn't have to find a better job because of it, how they didn't have to worry about medical bills, and somehow Gary was the one getting stuck paying all the bills when they went out to dinner or to the places they had wanted to take the kids to. All because they had the "extra income given to them". Gary felt that they had taken advantage of him, but he couldn't confront them with his feelings. Little did they know that Gary and Sadie were struggling to stay afloat because of the extra spending sprees brought on by having to pay for everything. It didn't seem to matter to anyone of them either.

Sadie and Gary had thought it would change after a while, but it hadn't. One night when they were all together at Gary's parent's place, his one brother made another comment about the extra free income that Gary received, and that was when Gary had told him to knock it off. But he continued to make the rude comments one right after another that night.

Sadie had thought his brother was rude, and maybe a little on the jealous side. That night when they got home Gary told Sadie that he had enough of his brothers comments, and of the whole family in general. He wasn't happy being around them or hearing about them anymore. He was furious with everything. Gary had thought Sadie was happy being close to family so he never brought it up to her until he had had enough of the rude comments. He had even thought it would break the two of them apart if it had continued. He was so torn and upset, and he wasn't sure what to do.

That was when Gary started to look into other jobs on the internet back where he was always happy. Happy when they had company, for the friends they had, his job he had in the military, and where they had lived in this small community. Once he had gotten the word that he was chosen for the job he wanted at the base, they had started packing immediately. Sadie said they couldn't pack fast enough.

They told their parents first, and they understood, but Gary and Sadie never told them about the comments being the reason why they weren't happy there. Once the rest of the family found out they were moving back, it was like turning a switch off with any of them coming around to visit anymore, especially by his brothers.

One time Gary ran into his one brother at the gas station where he made his last rude remark to Gary. He had wanted Gary to pay for his gas, since he had all that extra free money. Gary filled his own gas tank, and left without saying a word to him.

How sad I felt for them. They had moved back there to be close to everyone only to have it blow up in their face the way it had. It is really strange to think what others feel about their family members in the military. I was seeing and hearing stuff like this happening more often lately. Or maybe I was just listening more often instead of blabbing my mouth. But Charlie's family had been the same way towards him, too. And Matt's family just wanted him for his money. I just couldn't understand how family could be that way.

# EPILOGUE

⁕

Bradley did turn his life around for the good, and we were in contact with them at least once a week either through the church activities, the kids sport activities, or dance recitals for Charlotte Ann. Many times just visiting with each other and talking was enough for all of us. They have been included in all of our holiday traditions. Our friendship grew solid, and now we can talk easily about the past without the hate spewing from either one of us. I was glad to have them in our lives, and it made the holidays so much nicer.

Our kids had grown so fast, and have stayed in the area with their spouses and families. Mattie married Marie, and they have two kids, a boy and girl that are so precious. Yep, he married Sadie and Gary's daughter, Marie. When Mattie had finished college he came back to live in our town, and after seeing Marie all the time growing up as kids he had suddenly noticed she had also grew up, and was beautiful. Neither family had expected it, but we were both extremely happy for them.

Charlotte Ann married an attorney in town, and they also have two kids, a boy and a girl as well. Our family grew and the closeness we have is amazing the way Charlie and I had hoped it would happen, and so far I don't think we went wrong in that department.

As for our dear friend Helen… she sold her bed and breakfast, and moved to her daughter's place just a few years ago. Her bed and breakfast was too much for her to run by herself, and she refused to hire any help. She knew in her heart that it was time to retire. She was tired and wanted to be with her family as much as possible. She comes back every summer for two weeks staying with Charlie and me. She has been such a dear friend to all of us, and the kids to have a Nana-Helen. They loved her to pieces. She has made all my kids like her own grandchildren and a great Nana-Helen to my grandchildren. We couldn't have asked for any better of a grandmother for them either.

I think back about how fast Matt and I had met and married, meeting Helen the way we had, losing Matt, having Mattie that kept me going, buying the triplex, and meeting and marrying Charlie. My life has been a strange whirlwind with all the events that had unfolded, but if I had the chance to do it over again, I certainly would. My life has been filled with the most wonderful things anyone could ever want.

# THE END

# About The Author

## Joann Buie

Joann was born and raised in Ashtabula, Ohio, and liked writing short stories and numerous poems for others to read. Two hours after graduating from high school, she moved to Michigan to be with her husband, Bo, who was serving in the Air Force.

Moving to Arizona in 1979 as a young mother of three, Joann went to work in the school district in the Special Education department while completing her Bachelor's Degree. She earned her Master's Degree from Northern Arizona University while teaching elementary education.

After over twenty years working in the educational field and living over forty years in Arizona, she retired and now resides in Florida with her husband and two little dogs, Charlie Brown and Lucy.

Joann has been married for over fifty years, has three grown children and is a grandmother to seven.

Other Books in the

*Small Town Romance Series*

by

Joann Buie

# Abby's Quest

Abby struggled with her life right from the beginning by living in one foster home after another, until she graduated from high school. Everyone had referred to her as the basket baby that had been abandoned at a fire station after her birth, which was difficult for her to overcome.

Knowing she wanted to escape from there, and her past, to make a fresh start with her life in another town or state, she accepted a house sitting job in Jasper, Tennessee, not knowing what to expect or what would be waiting for her around the corner.

This heart warming romance story will leave you wanting to find out more about Abby's life, and how it had been changed along the way.

# Sandy Dunes Resort

Lexi had lost her dream job and her fiancee, Phillip, in New York City on the same day. Now, she was worried about her safety because of his indiscretions and of the illegal banking information she had stumbled upon that Phillip had been doing to his clients. The only thing she could do now was get out of New York City fast and stay under the radar of Phillip's rage. Lexi would now return to her family's home in Michigan, where she thought she would be safe from Phillip, only to have him track her there. Little did she know that her first love was working at the resort where she had lived with her Aunt Sandy.

On Lexi's return home, her life becomes an up-and-down battle. She battles with her old New York life that continues to haunt her, and the new life she is seeking keeps her in constant turmoil. As she tries to plan her future, she uncovers things from the past that happened during her college years that become so devastating to her that she thinks it may be in her best interest to just move away from all her family and friends.

Will Lexi find a future and the love she desires so desperately?

# Small Town Happiness

Sadie Stanton worked five years teaching fourth grade students, and loving it every minute. It was a career she had chosen ever since she was in the fourth grade, all because of the teacher she had that made learning enjoyable and achievable. Sadie wanted to be like her by making learning fun, and interesting for her students.

After teaching for five years Sadie was about to quit her teaching career. She had worked hard, and the kids responded with most of them reaching or exceeding the State Standards each year. The problem was that a lot of her co-workers resented her. They felt she was making them look bad, and that put a target on Sadie's back. It made the workplace very uncomfortable and a hostile place for Sadie, to say the least.

Not certain what it would be like if she was to leave what she thought was her dream job, and now not knowing if she would ever want to teach again, but she knew she couldn't stay there any longer.

Sadie knew she was ready to begin a new chapter in her life. She decided she would search for a new job, in a new town, and a new start.

Would Sadie find what she wanted all her life or maybe that life some how would find her.

# My Best Friend's Husband

Allison was a feisty little girl who thought she would be sent to live with her father. However, her plans didn't work out the and she ended up living in a home for children who had behavioral issues until she graduated from high school. Allison didn't have a mean streak in her body, but would act out in class enough to get sent to the principal's office every day. She was seeking attention, and she received it, but in a negative way. While living at that school, a counselor had befriended her during her senior year of high school helping her to receive a full scholarship to college. Allison was more than happy to leave Virginia behind, as well as her past, to begin a new life in Ohio.